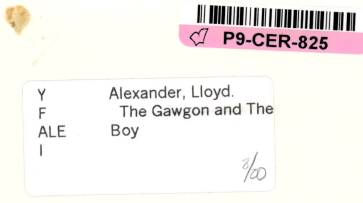

The Gawgon
and The BOY

Books by Lloyd Alexander

THE PRYDAIN CHRONICLES
The Book of Three
The Black Cauldron
The Castle of Llyr
Taran Wanderer
The High King
The Foundling

THE WESTMARK TRILOGY
Westmark
The Kestrel
The Beggar Queen

THE VESPER HOLLY ADVENTURES
The Illyrian Adventure
The El Dorado Adventure
The Drackenberg Adventure
The Jedera Adventure
The Philadelphia Adventure

OTHER BOOKS FOR YOUNG READERS
How the Cat Swallowed Thunder
Gypsy Rizka
The Iron Ring
The House Gobbaleen
The Arkadians

The Fortune-tellers
The Remarkable Journey of Prince Jen
The First Two Lives of Lukas-Kasha
The Town Cats and Other Tales
The Wizard in the Tree
The Cat Who Wished to Be a Man
The Four Donkeys
The King's Fountain
The Marvelous Misadventures of Sebastian
The Truthful Harp
Coll and His White Pig
Time Cat
The Flagship Hope: Aaron Lopez
Border Hawk: August Bondi
My Five Tigers

BOOKS FOR ADULTS
Fifty Years in the Doghouse
Park Avenue Vet (with Dr. Louis J. Camuti)
My Love Affair with Music
Janine Is French
And Let the Credit Go

TRANSLATIONS
Nausea, by Jean-Paul Sartre
The Wall, by Jean-Paul Sartre
The Sea Rose, by Paul Vialar
Uninterrupted Poetry, by Paul Eluard

The Gawgon
and The BOY

LLOYD ALEXANDER

DUTTON CHILDREN'S BOOKS | NEW YORK

For those with a Gawgon of their own,

and those who wish for one

Copyright © 2001 by Lloyd Alexander

Library of Congress Cataloging-in-Publication Data
Alexander, Lloyd.
The Gawgon and The Boy / by Lloyd Alexander.—1st ed.   p. cm.
Summary: In Depression-era Philadelphia, when eleven-year-old David is too ill
to attend school, he is tutored by the unique and adventurous Aunt Annie, whose
teaching combines with his imagination to greatly enrich his life.
ISBN 0-525-46677-0
[1. Imagination—Fiction.   2. Teacher-student relationships—Fiction.
3. Depressions—1929—Fiction.   4. Philadelphia (Pa.)—Fiction.]   I. Title.
PZ7.A3774 Gaw 2001   [Fic]—dc21   00-047541

Published in the United States by Dutton Children's Books,
a division of Penguin Putnam Books for Young Readers
345 Hudson Street, New York, New York 10014
www.penguinputnam.com

Designed by Amy Berniker
Printed in USA • First Edition
1   3   5   7   9   10   8   6   4   2

Contents

The Gawgon
and The BOY

{ Mother's side }

Grandfather	*m.*	Grandmother	Aunt Annie
(deceased)		Runs a boardinghouse featuring Nora the Parrot	"The Gawgon" (a distant cousin of my grandmother)

Will	Florry	Rosie	*m.*	Rob
"Uncle Santa Claus"	A nifty dresser and a swell dancer	Alarmed by microbes and the New Monia		Legal adviser and official turkey-carver

m. = married

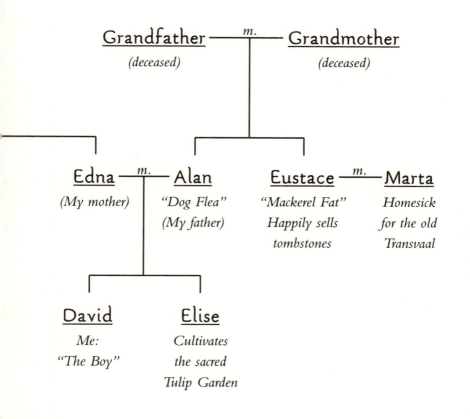

(Our Irish Shillelly)

§ Father's side §

Grandfather ———*m.*——— Grandmother
(deceased)   (deceased)

Edna ——*m.*—— Alan   Eustace ——*m.*—— Marta
(My mother)   "Dog Flea"   "Mackerel Fat"   Homesick
                (My father)   Happily sells   for the old
                                tombstones   Transvaal

David   Elise
Me: Cultivates
"The Boy"   the sacred
                 Tulip Garden

I

The Sea-Fox

When I first met The Gawgon, I never suspected who she was: climber of icy mountains, rescuer of King Tut's treasure, challenger of master criminals, and a dozen other things. But that came later, after I died—nearly died, anyhow.

"They really thought you were a goner," my sister said cheerfully. She had come to stand at my bedroom door. "What a nuisance you are."

In April of that year—one of those sour-tempered Philadelphia Aprils—I had the good luck to fall sick. I was delighted. Not that I enjoyed the worst part of it, but the best part was: It kept me out of school. Aside from a beehive buzzing in my head and a herd of weasels romping through my insides, I was beginning to feel pretty chipper.

No one told me straight out what ailed me. I was eleven

and had not reached complete visibility. My relatives, talking among themselves, tended to look through me—the Amazing Invisible Boy—or change the subject. I did overhear my mother and my aunt Rosie whispering in the hall about something Aunt Rosie called the New Monia. "Thank heaven it wasn't the Spanish Influenzo," she said to my mother. "Spaniards! What else will they send us?" Aunt Rosie lived in a state of eternal indignation and distrusted anything foreign.

"That's right, you nearly croaked," my sister happily went on. "Uncle Eustace was ready to sell us a tombstone."

Uncle Eustace, my father's brother, indeed sold tombstones for a living. As a result of sinus operations, deep scars crisscrossed his face. It made him look grim and somber, an advantage in his line of work.

"If I croaked"—I made frog noises—"it wouldn't bother me. I'd come back as a duppy and haunt you."

Duppy was the West Indian word for "ghost." I learned it from my father, born in Kingston, Jamaica. The prospect of meeting a duppy scared the wits out of him. Otherwise, he was completely fearless.

"There aren't any duppies in Philadelphia," my sister said. "So shut up about them. Just be glad you weren't quarantined."

I was not glad. I was disappointed. I would have liked one of those red or yellow stickers plastered on the front door, a badge of distinction. We still lived in the house on Lorimer Street then, and I had seen a few go up in the neighborhood, usually for measles, chicken pox, diphtheria (the Dip Theory,

Aunt Rosie called it). Every so often a boy suddenly vanished as if the goblins had got him. The black-lettered warning would appear, then a few days later, the boy himself, grinning behind the windowpane, his face magnificently blotched—almost as good as being tattooed. What was done with girls, I had no idea. They were a tribe apart.

I knew my sister was frantic over the possibility of a quarantine. No one could have gone in or out except the adults and our family physician, Dr. McKelvie. She would have been confined to quarters along with me. She was seventeen, and it would have devastated her Tulip Garden.

The Tulip Garden was the name I gave her circle of girlfriends, all looking much alike with their bobbed hairdos of chestnut, auburn, blond on slender necks. Their meetings were forbidden to me. I could only lurk in the hall while, behind her bedroom door, the Tulip Garden whispered and giggled. Separated, they would have withered; or their hair might have fallen out in despair. When no quarantine was needed, my sister grew more kindly disposed toward me.

"You're going to be all right, blighter," she said. She held her nose and stepped away from the door. "Pee-you. What do you do in here?"

She hurried to her room as if legions of my germs might attack her.

As for what I did: Apart from reading everything I could lay hands on, my favorite occupation was making up stories and drawing pictures to go with them. Before coming down sick, I

had taken a fancy to piracy, gorging myself on *Treasure Island,*
Captain Blood, and *The Sea-Hawk.* Now sitting up again, I went
back to the high seas.

My mind began drifting. The Spanish Influenza got mixed
up with the Spanish Main, with quarantines, duppies, Uncle
Eustace, and my grandmother's green parrot, Nora. The best pirates had beautiful ladies to worship from afar. I did not. I had
only begun to suspect that girls were interesting beings. But I
remembered my Jamaican cousin Allegra—we had, the year before, taken a trip to Kingston. Golden-skinned, with a peach
and turpentine fragrance of mangoes, she would, I thought, be
just fine.

THE SEA-FOX

*T*he Sea-Fox stood at the railing of the quarterdeck, his trusty
parrot, Nora, on his shoulder, a spyglass to his eye. Who would
have guessed this slim, steel-sinewed youth, captain of the most
dreaded pirate ship to sail the Spanish Main, was the son of
Lord Aldine, England's grandest nobleman?

A curious fate had set him on this course. Stricken by a terrible case of the New Monia, he had been sent on a sea voyage
to regain his health.

"No member of this family has had a sick day since the
Norman Conquest," declared his father. "Off you go, you puny
blighter. Never set foot in this manor again till you're fit to
wrestle a bear."

Months later, sailing homeward strong and vigorous, he was sorry to end the happy life he had found on the open sea. But then, nearly in sight of England's bleak and rainy shore, pirates attacked—"Avast! Belay!"—boarded his vessel, and swarmed over the deck.

Now lithe and muscular as a tiger, and handsomely suntanned, the lad fought so ferociously, to the wonder and admiration of friend and foe alike, that he was unanimously acclaimed—"Hip-hip hooray!"—captain of the buccaneers. All hands turned pirate, eager to serve under his command. From that day, he and his loyal crew became the terror of the sea-lanes; his good ship *Allegra* could overtake any sluggish merchantman—"Surrender, you lubbers! Join us or walk the plank."

Lord Aldine assumed the boy had either died at sea—proving a flaw in his son's character; or the ship had sunk—proving incompetence on the part of the shipmaster. Had the noble lord the slightest inkling of his son's profession, he would have exploded with purple rage.

The Sea-Fox narrowed his gaze on Kingston harbor: the green hills under a cloudless blue sky; the coconut palms and mango trees swaying in the warm breeze; taverns and storehouses clustering at the waterfront; the governor's gleaming white mansion rising above the town.

He smiled with satisfaction and called for the bosun, a grizzled old sea dog, brow and cheekbones crisscrossed by cutlass scars and a bad sinus condition.

"Mr. Eustace," ordered the Sea-Fox, "strike the Jolly Roger."

"Haul down the skull and bones? Aarr, Cap'n, what's afoot?"

"Then run up the yellow flag. Quarantine. Pestilence aboard."

"But, Cap'n"—the puzzled bosun frowned—"there's not even a case of measles. Except for Dr. McKelvie, the ship's surgeon, seasick as usual, we're hale and hearty, all the rest."

"Exactly."

When the Sea-Fox explained his plan, Mr. Eustace grinned and tugged a forelock: "Aye, a sweet little scheme. Aarr, Cap'n, they don't call ye Sea-Fox for nowt. And so we take the town, is it?"

"Kingston?" The Sea-Fox laughed. "Mr. Eustace, we shall take the whole island."

The bosun's face lit up. "Aarr, then we loot, sack, rifle, pillage—"

"Whatever amuses you. Seize the jewels, gold, ginger ale, and all the mangoes. Spare only the governor's mansion."

The Sea-Fox again turned his spyglass landward to focus on the upper floor of the building where Allegra, the governor's golden-skinned niece, had stepped onto the balcony.

"As for plunder, Mr. Eustace, divide it equally among the crew. But," the Sea-Fox murmured, "one priceless gem is mine."

2

The Cupped Boy

Next morning, I felt a lot less chipper. My eyelids seemed to be glued shut; I spent some time and effort getting them open. I had thrashed around during the night, the bedclothes were in a tangled mess on the floor; even without them I sweltered. My mother, meantime, must have called Dr. McKelvie; for here he was, big, cheerful, and smelling like Listerine.

"Well, now, laddie-buck, let's have a look at you." Dr. McKelvie dressed always in a black suit; a broad expanse of vest supported a gold watch and chain. His beard wreathed the bottom half of his face; it made me think of a bird's nest and I would not have been too surprised to see a cuckoo, like the one in my grandmother's clock, pop out of it.

While my mother hovered, Dr. McKelvie went about his

ritual of sticking a thermometer under my tongue, thumping my chest, listening through his stethoscope as if he were getting radio messages.

After that, there was talk about something to do with a hospital.

"Certainly not," my mother said. "Put him in with a crowd of sick people? To catch who knows what else?"

"Dear lady, in my considered opinion—"

"In *my* considered opinion," my mother said, "I know how to look after my own child."

Most people would have been overawed by Dr. McKelvie, for he took up a lot of space. My mother was overawed by no one. She went on in a pleasant tone but one not to be contradicted.

"Out of the question. A hospital will do more harm than good. No, he is in the best of hands." Under her breath, she added, "Mine."

My mother, alarmed, must have telephoned my father, for he came home much earlier than usual. He had no difficulty getting time off, since he ran his own business in center city: a store that sold Oriental goods. He took me there on the occasional Saturday and I loved it: a treasure house smelling of joss sticks and incense, crowded with paper lanterns, screens, lamps, vases, and jewelry. He once had been a stockbroker. Why he quit and chose this exotic profession, I never knew; unless it simply amused him.

He came to bend over me. He wore elegant pince-nez glasses which I expected to fall off at any moment, but they always stayed clamped to the bridge of his nose. "How are you, Bax old sport?"

"Bax" was his latest nickname for me. I had no idea where or why he came up with it. Names in our family were flexible. While my sister Elise and I addressed our parents as "Mother" and "Father," other titles came up on the spur of the moment and stuck until new ones replaced them. Some stayed permanent. Though my mother always called my father by his proper name, Alan, he called her "Ed" or "Eddie." He still called his brother Eustace by his Jamaican boyhood nickname, "Mackerel Fat" and was, in turn, addressed as "Dog Flea."

Of names, I enjoyed more than my share. To Dr. McKelvie, I was "laddie-buck." To my sister, "blighter." To my various relatives, I was at one time or another "Skeezix," "Skinamalink," or "Snicklefritz." Only my mother called me by my given name, David.

To his question, I insisted I was fine.

"Of course you are," my father said.

My mother motioned with her head, and they went out into the hall.

For the next couple of days, I was too foggy to be interested in much of anything. But I did perk up enough to try drawing pictures, imitating the cartoon panels I saw in the comic strips, and went back to Kingston, where I had left the Sea-Fox.

THE SEA-FOX CLAIMS HIS PRIZE

Mr. Eustace, as ordered, had run up the yellow flag to signal pestilence aboard. The *Allegra* drifted closer to the harbor. Consternation reigned along the waterfront. The townsfolk crowded the wharves, shaking their fists and warning the plague-ridden vessel to stand away. A boat was launched and rowed within a safe distance from the ship. The harbormaster, standing in the bow, commanded the *Allegra* to turn about and sail as far as possible out to sea.

"Aarr, it can't be done," Mr. Eustace called through a speaking trumpet.

"It demmed well better be," flung back the harbormaster, "else we open fire on you."

The *Allegra*'s crew, meantime, had hidden themselves well out of sight. Mr. Eustace repeated, "Can't be done, no matter."

Silently watchful on the quarterdeck, the Sea-Fox—who never told a lie—had assigned the bosun—who never told the truth—this deceptive but necessary task:

"No hands to work the ship," declared Mr. Eustace. "They're dead, all but me and the cap'n. Died of the Spanish Influenzo; bloated bellies, running sores, that kind of thing."

"Dead! Awk, awk!" Nora bounced up and down on the shoulder of the Sea-Fox. "Every man jack, dead as doorknobs."

"No business of mine." The harbormaster held a handkerchief to his nose. "Don't come near. Can't work the ship? Then drift out to sea on the night tide. Drift to the devil, for all I care."

"Aye, aye," replied the bosun, "so we'll do."

At midnight, following his plan, the Sea-Fox ordered the jolly boats lowered over the side. The *Allegra* carried a number of these small, light craft for just such occasions. With muffled oars, the Sea-Fox leading, the jolly boats skimmed swiftly to the sleeping harbor.

The crew, also according to plan, had draped themselves in lengths of sailcloth. Reaching the docks, they clambered ashore and gave voice to bloodcurdling shrieks. The drowsy watchman, rousing, gaped in terror.

"Duppies!" he bawled. "Hundreds! Duppies everywhere!"

Seeing the white-shrouded figures, convinced the town had been invaded by the ghosts of diseased sailors, the entire population raced for the hills. Adding to the panic, the crew smashed many huge barrels of ginger ale, and the amber liquid gushed in rivers down the streets. Warehouses were broken into, thousands of mangoes rolled in all directions.

The Sea-Fox, discarding his ghostly disguise, strode to the governor's mansion. Unchallenged, he climbed the marble staircase and halted at a bedchamber door. With one mighty kick from his booted foot, he shattered it from its hinges.

Allegra turned toward him. Months before, the Sea-Fox had boarded a vessel carrying her, the governor, and his lady to Jamaica. Ordinarily, the Sea-Fox would have set the passengers adrift. However, the sparkle in Allegra's eyes betokened more than passing interest and held a promise for the future.

"We shall meet again," he whispered in her shell-like ear.

Now here she was, her face aglow with the same illumination he had seen at their first encounter.

"You idiot," she said, "why did you kick down my door? It was unlatched; I was waiting for you. At least," she added, "you could have knocked."

The Sea-Fox nodded acceptance of this gentle reproof. He pointed at the town below, where his loyal crew were guzzling ginger ale and stuffing themselves with mangoes.

"Kingston is mine. And yours," he said. "I mean to declare Jamaican independence. The grateful population will acclaim us president and first lady. Or king and queen, if you prefer. We shall occupy this splendid residence—"

"Have you lost your mind?" Allegra burst out. "Gone stark raving bonkers? Why do you suppose I waited for you? To stay on some boring island? Besides, I hate mangoes. I say we haul out of here, back to the high seas, plundering merchantmen, sinking frigates."

"Then so we shall!" happily exclaimed the Sea-Fox, who had not really looked forward to life ashore. "Yes, the two of us will terrify the Spanish Main together."

"My Sea-Fox!" cried Allegra.

"My pirate bride!" he answered.

"Your Sea-Vixen," said Allegra.

———————

Later, my sister came to announce confidentially: "You're going to be cupped."

I had no idea what she meant. Put into a cup? It would have to be a large one.

"Grandmother phoned. She told Mother it would be a good idea. They did it to me once," she added. "It was disgusting and weird. Just the kind of thing you like. They're calling Mrs. Jossbegger."

This puzzled me. I knew Mrs. Jossbegger, a woman of some bulk who wheezed a lot. She had, so far as I could tell, nothing to do with cups. She made her living from feet: cutting ladies' toenails and paring their corns.

Mrs. Jossbegger made regular visits to Larchmont Street, where my grandmother kept a boardinghouse. On those occasions, my mother and my various aunts gathered in the parlor. We all lived within a few blocks of each other, so it was an easy walk.

I was always glad to be taken along. At the boardinghouse, something was always going on: lodgers coming in and out, meals being cooked, a cluttered cellar I was allowed to explore. And, above all, Nora the parrot.

Nora had been left behind when one of the lodgers furtively departed still owing a good amount of back rent. Now she lived in the parlor, free to perch on her T-shaped pole or do acrobatics on top of her cage.

I never missed a chance to talk with her, though what she said was mainly gibberish, with a lot of squawking and whistling. Sometimes she did come out with understandable sentences:

"We're all drunk but Nora," she warbled, adding noises like breaking glass. Then she whooped and giggled. "Naughty boy, get your hand off my leg. Hoorah, hoorah!"

I could only guess at the life she had led before settling into the boardinghouse.

The corn-cutting sessions were social events as much as they were podiatric treatments. Awaiting Mrs. Jossbegger, the ladies gathered in a circle, a grown-up Tulip Garden, drinking tea and gossiping.

Also attending was one of the two permanent residents: Aunt Annie (an honorary title, she was my grandmother's distant cousin), thin as a stick, always in floor-length black skirts, her white hair twisted into a bun. Although she hobbled downstairs for meals and other important happenings, she had never to my knowledge set foot outside the boardinghouse. The other permanent resident was Captain Jack—not a real captain, we called him that because it pleased him. Shell-shocked in the Great War, he never left his room at all; except, from time to time, when he went sleepwalking.

I admired Captain Jack as a great hero. His sleepwalking also fascinated me, and I wished I, too, could be a sleepwalker. I liked visiting with him and listening to his gramophone records. To him, I was "First Sergeant," and we were fond friends.

Aunt Annie, however, seemed a grim and forbidding presence. Not that she treated me with anything less than kindness. To her credit, at Christmas and my birthdays, when my relatives usually gave me handkerchiefs and underwear, she gave me books. Still, she made me uneasy. Invisibility has its advantages; but when she turned her sharp glances on me, watching me closely, I was no longer the Amazing Invisible Boy. On the contrary, I felt she could see me very clearly indeed and quite possibly could read my mind. For that reason, she frightened me a little. Or perhaps it was simply because she was very old.

Nevertheless, I saw no connection between corn cutting and being cupped. So, that evening, when Mrs. Jossbegger came wheezing into my room, I was curious, eager to know what she intended to do, and maybe a touch apprehensive. My sister holed up in her own quarters; my father preferred staying downstairs. My mother stripped off my pajama top while Mrs. Jossbegger set half a dozen globes like small fishbowls on the night table.

Flat on my stomach, my mother more or less squashing down my head, I could not see precisely what was going on. From the corner of my eye, I glimpsed Mrs. Jossbegger setting fire to a cotton ball on a stick. I braced myself, suspecting she planned on setting me alight as well. Instead, heating the inside of the globes, she planted them in rows along my back, where they stuck as if glued there. I was commanded not to move. After a time, Mrs. Jossbegger pulled off the globes; they came away with a pop like the rubber suction cups on toy arrows.

"Would you look at that?" she whispered to my mother. "Black as ink. There's all the bad blood coming out."

I was allowed, with a hand mirror, to admire the result.

Dark bumps like giant mosquito bites covered my back; a spectacular effect. I was as proud as if I had received tribal initiation marks like those I had seen in *National Geographic*.

Mrs. Jossbegger nodded professional satisfaction. My mother gave me a drink of something that smelled like mothballs. Of course, blessedly, I had no hint then of what would catch us all up and shatter us. Without a thought even for the Sea-Fox, I slept happily, dreamlessly.

3

The Back-Alley Gang

Mrs. Jossbegger's cups and Dr. McKelvie's foul-tasting concoctions must have combined to good effect. Despite a couple of setbacks, when I felt as if I were going down the wrong end of a telescope, by the end of May I was out of bed some of the time, ready to receive visiting aunts and uncles.

An outsider would have been bewildered by the array of relatives and lost in the tangled branches of the family tree. But I had known them all my life, knew them as I knew the fingers of my hand, and had no trouble sorting them out. They were, in sum, the family.

I saw little of my father's brother Eustace—my tombstone uncle. He was busy reading the death notices in the morning papers and hurrying out to drum up customers. But his wife,

Marta, came by. Stout, ruddy-cheeked, she was born in South Africa and had been homesick ever since. I thought of her as my singing aunt, for she had a clear, beautiful voice. I begged her to sing her favorite, "Sari Marais," and joined in the yearning refrain:

> Oh, take me back to the old Transvaal,
> That's where I long to be.
> Down among the mealies
> And the green thorn trees . . .

Mealies, she explained as she tried to teach me the words in Afrikaans, were ears of corn. I had never seen a mealie or a green thorn tree, but the melody brought tears to my eyes each time I heard it. However, it vexed Uncle Eustace.

"Transvaal?" he would burst out, putting his hands to his shattered forehead. "Transvaal? What's wrong with Philadelphia?"

My grandmother came as often as she could leave the boardinghouse to itself. I thought she looked a little like George Washington in the portrait on my classroom wall, except she smiled more and her wrinkled cheeks turned pale pink when she threw back her head and laughed, which was frequently. She moistened her fingertips in her mouth and rubbed away smudges on my face, confident that grandmotherly saliva cured everything.

Aunt Rosie, of course, was always there, spreading alarm

about microbes drifting in through open windows; and warning my mother I could poke my eye out with a pencil when I bent over my sketch pad. Her husband, Rob, my mother's eldest brother, was the distinguished uncle. He had a job with the Pennsylvania Railroad.

So, I felt highly honored when Uncle Rob came in person to visit me.

"Here's a little something for you, Snicklefritz." Uncle Rob slipped me a quarter. He always and unfailingly slipped me a quarter each time we met. "I hear you're doing fine. You'll be back to school in no time."

In our family, Uncle Rob was the one who handled wills, last testaments, codicils, and all such grim and stifling business. Naturally, he would bring up the subject of school.

The mere mention of the word sent me into a sudden choking fit, and he had to go away. I had forgotten about school. It was the distant past, long out of my thoughts. Now that Uncle Rob had reminded me, I would have begged to be flogged, disemboweled, and forced to drink molten lead rather than returned to classes. I had some reluctance about being educated.

My sister did not seem to mind, which made me doubt her sanity. We both went to Rittenhouse Academy: she in Upper School, I in Middle School. The headmaster, Dr. Legg, a solemn figure in black academic robes, believed in plain living and high thinking, a sound mind in a sound body, those goals to be attained through cold showers and scratchy toilet paper.

The soundness of our bodies was enhanced by endless games of soccer. We turned out, rain or shine, in baggy white shorts and drooping athletic supporters, or exercised in the gymnasium, which smelled as if foxes lived there. To strengthen our minds, we plodded through our classes grimly fixated on each subject, never venturing on any exciting side trips. It felt like trudging down a rutted road. Yawning mentally, hypnotically bored, I paid barely enough attention to squeak by. Mainly, I drew pictures or penciled stick figures—"Skinny Pinnies"—on the margins of my textbooks.

Dr. Legg assured us, whenever he addressed the assembled school, that Rittenhouse Academy was preparing us for the great battle of life. We would be ready to conquer empires or run for Congress.

My father had more modest expectations. If I studied hard and seriously applied myself, he told me, I might, like Uncle Rob, get an office job with the Pennsylvania Railroad.

Whether Uncle Rob put the question into my mother's head or whether it occurred to her on her own, I did not know. But the next time Dr. McKelvie came, she asked him when I could go back to Rittenhouse Academy.

"My dear madam"—Dr. McKelvie chewed his beard for a moment—"you surely understand the boy has been gravely ill. Return to school? For what little remains of the term? No, surely not. Possibly not the fall term either. That remains to be seen. A lengthy convalescence, absolutely essential—"

"I won't have him turned into a shut-in," my mother said. "That simply won't do at all."

"I agree," Dr. McKelvie said. "School can wait, no rush about it. What I recommend is some fresh air, mild exercise." He turned to me. "How does that suit you, laddie-buck?"

I could have kissed his stethoscope.

Dr. McKelvie snatched me from the gallows. Had I known the consequences, I might have been more wary; but I cared only to be set loose for my "mild exercise" in the world. That is, the back-alley world of Lorimer Street; canyons of green-painted board fences, trash bins, garbage cans, tiny courtyards and areaways—"airy ways," Aunt Rosie called them. Hucksters pushed carts through the alleys, hawking berries, melons, vegetables. The passages were barely wide enough for the iceman's horse and wagon. When he reined up to chop out the glittering blocks, grappling them with iron tongs, to shoulder them into kitchen iceboxes, he was ambushed by knickered bandits seizing the frozen splinters, crunching them loudly or sucking them until they melted.

By the middle of June, I had gained a couple of henchmen who lived nearby: Deveraux, whose arms had grown faster than the rest of him and, as a result, did convincing imitations of a chimpanzee, hooting, grinning, scratching himself, scuffing his knuckles along the pavement; Barnick, spiky-haired, wearing knee-length boots, which I coveted, all the more since one boot had a sheath for a jackknife. We had, until then, seen little of each other; we became cronies nonetheless. They knew I went to private school, but good-natured fellows, they never held it against me.

I supplied them with cootie-catchers. Producing those items was one of my major skills, perfected while wool-gathering in class. Like Japanese origami, the cootie-catcher began with a square of paper folded in on itself a couple of times. Its construction let a boy (I never saw a girl use a cootie-catcher) hold it so that one inside surface was blank.

Passing the cootie-catcher through a victim's hair, then changing finger position, it appeared filled with lice and fleas (drawn there beforehand). By unspoken agreement, the one whose cooties had thus been caught was required to yell in disgust at the vermin found on his person. The joke had limitations. After a few times, the effect wore off, by the law of diminishing cootie returns. The only solution: to draw the creatures larger, more grotesque. After a time, nevertheless, the most nauseating roaches and giant bedbugs ceased to shock. Even Deveraux had to force himself, out of politeness, to hoot in mock terror.

I pondered improvements. My downfall began, as with so many artists, with a grand vision, a new conception. I was inspired to paint the cooties in vivid colors.

Uncle Rob, when last we met, had slipped me the ritual quarter. I intended buying paints. Where the back alleys ended, a miniature city included a barbershop, shoeshine parlor, drugstore with a marble soda fountain, and a movie house. A penny-candy store also offered small toys and art supplies. There, in artistic frenzy, I sacrificed all of Uncle Rob's quarter and bought a tin box of watercolors and a scraggy brush.

I was eager to take my purchases home, but Barnick and Deveraux wanted to see a movie; the neighborhood theater was showing one of the new films that actually talked. Deveraux produced a dime. Barnick dredged up three cents. I was already totally bankrupt. Much as I would have loved an afternoon movie, it was not possible. Pooling our resources came far short of the admission price for all of us. I saw no way around that hard financial fact.

Deveraux and Barnick looked at me with the tolerant amusement shown to puppies and idiots. They had a plan, simple and elegant. Deveraux would pay to get in. Barnick and I were to wait outside the fire exit, which Deveraux would open for us: a scheme worthy of the Sea-Fox.

Deveraux, winking and making chimpanzee faces, headed for the box office. Barnick and I crouched amid the trash barrels by the fire exit. Moments later, the door swung open just wide enough for us to squeeze through.

4

A Hardened Criminal

Sudden darkness blinded me, the bright silver screen dazzled me. I had taken no more than two steps into the half-empty theater when a figure loomed up. Barnick yelled, I tried to dodge aside. A hand clamped the scruff of my neck. Collared likewise, Barnick was thrashing around beside me. The usher, triumphant in a pillbox hat and brass buttons, hustled us through the movie house. The flickering figures on the screen kept on talking, laughing, and tap-dancing heedless of our fate.

Deveraux had streaked away into the shadows of the aisles. We thought no less of him for his desertion; he could do nothing but save himself. Hopeless prisoners, we were marched up a flight of iron steps into a tiny office.

The windowless room stank of cigar smoke and celluloid

film. At a cluttered table, arm garters on his sleeves, hair slicked down with Vaseline and parted in the middle, the manager congratulated our captor, dismissed him, and turned a fish eye on us.

"What's this, eh? I'd say we've got a couple of fine young hoodlums here." Mr. Kardon—I later learned this was his despicable name—got up to strut back and forth like a bantam rooster. "Now, you little thugs, what's to be done with you? Want to guess? No? I'll tell you, then. Make an example of you. Hooligans like you sneaking in here—I'm fed up with it. Barefaced thievery, money out of my pocket. Next, you'll rob me at gunpoint. So, it's police business now. Oh, yes, the station house for you. In handcuffs. Behind bars, where you belong."

Barnick started blubbering. I tried to assume a scornful attitude—the Sea-Fox in the clutches of the enemy—but I was blubbering as well, no doubt louder than Barnick.

Mr. Kardon blustered and browbeat us awhile, then demanded our telephone numbers. He did not call the police. Worse, he called our mothers.

We stood waiting, sniffling, not daring to wipe our eyes and noses. Mr. Kardon had caught sight of the jackknife in Barnick's boot and confiscated it. When Mrs. Barnick arrived, he went through the sorry tale of our crime.

"And this? What's this?" Mr. Kardon pried open the evidence to reveal a broken-tipped blade. "A lethal weapon."

My mother, meantime, had come into the office and the whole business started up again.

"Call them children?" Mr. Kardon folded his arms. "I'll tell you what they are. A disgrace to their families. Bad to worse if they keep on like this. Hardened criminals."

Mr. Kardon ranted on about a life of crime, jailbirds, a road to the penitentiary, a strong likelihood of the electric chair—at this, he eyed me directly, as if seeing me (as I saw myself) strapped into that particular item of furniture. He finally got tired and decided to grant clemency.

We were paroled into the custody of our mothers. Mrs. Barnick hustled her son from the office. Beyond the door, I could hear Barnick having his head smacked.

I was fidgeting to be gone. Mr. Kardon sat down at his table and shuffled papers. My mother did not budge. She bent forward and said, almost in a whisper: "You miserable little man, how dare you? How dare you call my son a criminal? Jailbird? Prison? This is outrageous. You, sir, should be the one behind bars for your atrocious behavior."

The Vaseline on Mr. Kardon's hair seemed to melt. My mother dipped into her purse and took out a quarter.

"This"—she set the coin on the table—"will more than pay his admission. You may keep the change."

As we walked home, I steeled myself to be scolded. My mother said not a word, as if the shameful event had never happened. When my father came home and we all sat down to dinner, she still mentioned nothing about it. We were all in a good mood. Relieved, I sped to my room.

Later, my sister poked her head in. "You got caught, didn't you? That's what happens to sneaky little blighters."

Surprised, I asked how she knew.

"Oh, I know," she said. "The whole thing. They were talking after you went upstairs."

I had no reason to doubt her. Unlike myself, the Amazing Invisible Boy, she was totally visible at all times, counted as a young lady, and thus privy, if not specifically invited, to adult conversations. She was always glad to pass along disagreeable information.

"They're going to do something to you," she said.

I asked what it was.

"They aren't sure." She shrugged. "They're thinking about it. You're not getting off, you know. Whatever it is, you're not going to like it."

She wished me a cheery good night.

I tried to imagine what punishments would be inflicted. Confinement, hard labor, exile—none of them absolutely unbearable. Besides, I judged myself relatively blameless. Uncle Rob was at the root of it. If he hadn't given me the quarter, I wouldn't have spent it. If I hadn't spent it, I'd have had money for legal admission. If I'd paid to get in, I wouldn't have been grabbed by a pimply-faced usher decked out like an organ grinder's monkey and threatened with electrocution by a cock-of-the-walk with Vaseline on his head. Still, the nameless, shapeless "something" hung over me. The Sea-Fox, meantime, was having his own troubles.

THE SEA-FOX IN CHAINS

Shackled hand and foot, the Sea-Fox lay on the damp straw of his cell in Portsmouth Prison. Through the grated window trickled the busy clatter of the waterfront and the stench of bodies hanging in chains at Execution Dock. For all that, he kept a calm spirit. When last seen, Mr. Eustace the bosun, Dr. McKelvie the ship's surgeon, and the rest of the crew, urged on by Nora the parrot, were in the jolly boats rowing away as fast as their arms could work the oars.

Treachery and deception had led him to this dismal cell. A week before, he had sighted a lazy merchantman ripe for plucking. Sea-Vixen at the helm, the *Allegra* closed rapidly with the vessel.

"All hands on deck! Prepare to board!" the Sea-Fox commanded.

"Sink the lubbers!" Nora crowed gleefully. "Yo-ho! Awk, awk!"

No sooner did the *Allegra* come alongside than the merchantman hoisted the white flag of surrender. With the ships hull to hull, the Sea-Fox sprang lightly over the railing to the deck of the captured prize. The captain, a puffed-up little man, hair slick with Vaseline, approached to offer his sword in submission. As the Sea-Fox reached for it, a company of seagoing constables, pimply-faced, in pillbox hats and brass-buttoned uniforms, burst up from the hatches. Royal Navy gunners ran out cannon disguised as innocent pieces of hardware and fired point-blank at the helpless *Allegra*.

"Shameful treachery!" the Sea-Fox indignantly exclaimed. "Is this conduct worthy of an officer and gentleman?"

"Heh-heh-heh," sneered the captain. "You plundered Kingston, made off with every mango on the island, and stole the governor's niece. We've been on your trail ever since."

"Save yourselves!" the Sea-Fox shouted to the crew. "Into the jolly boats!"

The struggling Allegra was taken in hand by the constables and led to a cabin. The Sea-Fox was immediately clapped in irons.

"You'll swing for this," declared the gloating captain. "I'll see you dance on the gallows, you hardened criminal!"

When the First Lord of the Admiralty learned Allegra's true identity as the governor's niece, he instantly pardoned and set her free. The Sea-Fox, never breathing a word of his noble parentage, languished in a cell until hauled into court to stand in the prisoners' dock.

"You have no possible defense, not the slightest mitigating circumstance that will save you from condemnation," declared the white-wigged, red-robed judge while the Sea-Fox maintained a dignified silence. "The jury"—he gestured at the grim faces in the box—"will hardly need to withdraw to determine a verdict." He reached for his black velvet cap, signifying a sentence of death.

"Milord!" a familiar voice rang out. "I submit overriding evidence!"

Allegra, now charmingly gowned, swept her way to the bar of justice.

"I have consulted with the directors of the Bank of England." A hush fell over the spectators at the mention of this sacred institution; Allegra held up a sheaf of papers.

"The figures are indisputable. The depredations of this gallant Sea-Fox have devastated the whole Spanish economy. Spain has become too impoverished to threaten anyone, least of all Great Britain."

"Commendable that may be," replied the judge, "but the Sea-Fox has also plundered English merchantmen."

"Yes, from time to time," admitted Allegra. "Not enough to matter. Without competition from Spain, Britannia rules the waves, and prosperity reigns throughout the British Isles.

"Until now, England faced financial ruin," Allegra went on. "No longer. The Sea-Fox has saved the British Empire from bankruptcy."

"Good heavens, I had no idea this was the state of affairs." The judge flung away his black cap and turned to the Sea-Fox. "This case, I am happy to declare, is dismissed. You are free to go, accompanied by the thanks of a grateful nation."

The spectators burst into cheers and threw their hats in the air. The jurymen streamed from the box to hoist Allegra and the Sea-Fox onto their shoulders and bear them from the courtroom.

"Brilliantly argued," remarked the Sea-Fox to Allegra. "You saved my life—but what if the judge had not accepted your defense? What if the case had gone to the jury and they chose to convict me?"

"I took that remote possibility into account," said Allegra, "and used my considerable influence as the governor's niece to guard against it. The Lord Chief Justice himself allowed me to pick the jury; and the jury—*this* jury would have never found you guilty."

The jurymen began pulling off false beards and mustaches, green spectacles, and cardboard noses, revealing themselves as Mr. Eustace, Dr. McKelvie, and others of the Sea-Fox's loyal crew, including Nora the parrot.

"Justice has prevailed," said the Sea-Fox.

"With a little help," said the Sea-Vixen.

The *Allegra* had gone into dry dock for repairs; the crew waited eagerly to set sail again as soon as the vessel was shipshape. One duty remained.

Once more in England, the Sea-Fox thought it only correct to present Allegra to his noble father. The happy couple rode to Aldine Manor in a golden coach and four, a gift from the grateful Board of Trade, and entered the baronial hall. Lord Aldine, surrounded by suits of armor and ancestral portraits, sat drinking a glass of vintage root beer.

"My dear father," said the Sea-Fox, "I have returned home."

"Gadzooks! So you have." Lord Aldine blinked. "Not drowned after all? Bit of a surprise, wot? Didn't you used to be a puny sort of blighter?"

"Allegra and I seek your blessing," said the Sea-Fox, "which we pray you will grant."

"Zounds! Nothing would please me more, haw, haw! Handsome pair you make, new branch on the old family tree—" Lord Aldine stopped and raised a hand. "Here, now, just a minute. I distinctly recall telling you never to set foot in this manor until you were fit to wrestle a bear."

The Sea-Fox bowed gracefully. "I stand ready to fulfill that condition."

Lord Aldine ordered a footman to lead in a huge bear from his private zoo. Allegra gasped at the sight of the gigantic animal, but the face of the Sea-Fox brightened.

"Bruno!" he cried. "How you've grown!"

The eyes of the bear also lit up, recognizing his old playmate. Since he was a cub, Bruno and the young Sea-Fox had romped over the meadows of the estate.

The Sea-Fox and the bear held out their arms to each other. Instead of wrestling, however, the two began dancing happily, whirling around the great hall.

"Good enough!" exclaimed Lord Aldine. "Right-o! I give you my blessings and welcome to them."

Allegra stepped to the side of the smiling bear.

"May I have the next waltz?" she said.

━━━━━━━━━━━━━━━━━━ **Thuh End** ━━━━━━━━━━━━━━━━

As for the "something" my sister warned lay in store for me, I was present when it was revealed.

My mother had taken me to my grandmother's boarding-house for Mrs. Jossbegger's corn-cutting session. I fed Nora grapes; the ladies chatted as usual, though in a different, more earnest tone. I had gone totally invisible and was probably considered deaf as well. I heard Aunt Rosie, paying no attention to whether I was there or not, say: "Of course, he can't be allowed to run the streets like a savitch. You see the mischief he got into. Bad company. Rotten apples."

"A childish prank," my mother said. "I wouldn't call Mrs. Deveraux's son a rotten apple; Mrs. Barnick's, either."

"With a knife in his boot?" Aunt Rosie countered.

"I don't want things to get out of hand," my mother admitted. "He's missed too much school already, and likely to miss more. Dr. McKelvie was very uncertain about that."

Aunt Rosie clicked her tongue. "He could turn out to be some kind of ignoramiss."

"Alan and I thought the vicar could help," my mother said. "He might suggest someone to give private lessons."

"A tooter?" said Aunt Rosie.

"Something like that," said my mother, and my grandmother nodded agreement. "Maybe Mr. Milliken, the Sunday-school teacher. He seems to be a pleasant sort of fellow. Or a university student in his spare time. I suppose, if we had to, we could put a classified advertisement in the paper."

Aunt Rosie snorted. "The public press? You never know what you'll fish up."

My heart chilled as they went on calmly discussing my fate. One way or another, I was doomed to be removed from the back alley. A private teacher? One person, face-to-face, with a constant eye on me? Worse than Rittenhouse Academy, where I could hide unnoticed among my classmates.

Aunt Annie, silent until now, put down her cup. In a tone that made me think of the Almighty commanding Abraham to sacrifice young Isaac, she said:

"Give me the boy."

5

The Gawgon

"Why, Annie, that's a fine idea," my mother said. "It never occurred to me. If you feel up to it—"

"I've dealt with harder cases." Aunt Annie gave me a glance which included me in that category.

"I'll talk to Alan," my mother said. "We'll work out the details."

No one asked the Amazing Invisible Boy's opinion. I would have told them that if I was doomed to be educated, I preferred a total stranger, one I could shirk, dodge, and bamboozle. Aunt Annie saw me all too clearly. My animal instinct warned me that she was not to be bamboozled.

I expected the plan would go into immediate effect. But for the next several days, no one said anything more. I hoped it had been forgotten or, when consulted, my father had rejected it.

Meanwhile, I had no heart for the charms of the back alley. Barnick and Deveraux had been banished to summer camp in the Poconos. Their punishment: to play baseball, swim in lakes, ride horses, and toast marshmallows.

I hoped Aunt Rosie, indignant about everything else, would come up with overpowering objections. She did not, though I heard her remark, later, to my mother:

"She was a hellion in her younger days, you know. Oh, I'll bet she can still be a real gawgon."

Whatever a hellion was did not sound promising. Gawgon—by that I understood Aunt Rosie meant "gorgon." I knew about gorgons, and Medusa, a horrible monster with snakes for hair, the sight of whom turned everybody to stone. The hero Perseus slew her, cleverly looking only at her reflection in his polished shield. This I gleaned from a book of Greek mythology The Gawgon herself had given me as a birthday gift. ("The Gawgon" was now my secret name for Aunt Annie. It had a ring more sinister than "gorgon.")

Desperate, I prayed the government would step in and save me when I heard my father say something about approval from the Board of Education. But it turned out The Gawgon had a certificate that made everything legal.

My mother outlined the schedule: classes on Monday, Wednesday, and Friday afternoons. Then, a special treat: Saturdays, I could sleep overnight at the boardinghouse.

That, in itself, was worth a few miserable hours with The

Gawgon. I could visit Captain Jack, talk to Nora, explore the cellar, wind up the cuckoo clock, and eat pancakes on Sunday morning.

As I told my sister, I looked forward to the weekend holidays.

"You really are a stupid blighter," said my sister, who claimed to understand the twisted minds of adults. "It's a chance for Mother and Father to get you out of the house. Holiday? Yes. For them."

The Monday following, my mother deposited me at the boardinghouse. I had been outfitted with composition books, paper, pens, and pencils. Thus heavily armed, I cautiously made my way upstairs to The Gawgon's lair.

I ran into Dr. McKelvie coming down the hall. He clapped me on the shoulder, addressed me as "laddie-buck," and said he was glad to see me on the mend. I supposed he had been visiting Captain Jack, but the door was shut and Captain Jack was playing his gramophone.

I went on to The Gawgon's den. The room was crowded, but neatly crowded, with a rolltop desk and cluttered pigeonholes, a dresser and oval mirror, bookcases, a narrow bed, an electric lamp on the night table. For a den, it was fairly sunny, with pale light from the window that overlooked the street. A card table had been unfolded, waiting. The Gawgon sat in a rocking chair. She motioned with her head.

"Doctors is all swabs," she remarked as I entered. Until now, I had never noticed her eyes were a bright, frosty blue. "Who said that?"

"Why—you did, Aunt." I had not expected such a comment or question. "Just now."

"No, no, boy. Who else? In a book I gave you at Christmas."

Things were not beginning well. I thought hard for a while. Something stirred; it came to me.

"Billy Bones? In *Treasure Island*?"

The Gawgon nodded. "Who wrote it? A Scotsman," she went on as I shrugged, having forgotten. "Robert Louis Stevenson. You should always remember authors' names. Out of courtesy; poor devils, they haven't much else to hang on to.

"He wrote it for a boy about your age," she added. "To amuse him. Did it amuse you?"

"Yes," I cautiously admitted, suspecting some kind of Gawgon-ish trap.

"Stevenson wrote a good many of his books in bed, did you know that? He was very sick. Oh, a lot sicker than you were. He went to live in Samoa, at the end. They called him *Tusitala*—'storyteller.' When he died, they buried him in the mountains. He wrote this—it's on his gravestone:

> *Under the wide and starry sky,*
> *Dig the grave and let me lie.*
> *Glad did I live and gladly die,*
> * And I laid me down with a will.*

This be the verse you grave for me:
Here he lies where he longed to be;
Home is the sailor, home from the sea,
And the hunter home from the hill.

The Gawgon had been looking beyond the window. She glanced back at me:

"Do you understand any of that?"

I had to confess I did not. (Also, at the edge of my mind a picture briefly took shape: Uncle Eustace scrambling up the mountains of Samoa to sell Robert Louis Stevenson a tombstone.) I said I couldn't see why anybody would be glad to die.

"Nor should you." The Gawgon brushed away an invisible gnat. "Not yet. Not yet," she said as much to herself as to me. "Pay me no mind," she added. "It's McKelvie, that cheerful undertaker. He puts morbid notions into people's heads."

She gestured for me to sit at the card table. "Let's see your hand . . . No, boy, your hand*writing*." I had raised a palm. "Use a new pen point."

I took a fresh steel nib from my box. Before fitting it into the wooden penholder, I put it into my mouth to suck away the coating film of oil, common practice at school.

"Are you trying to skewer your tongue?" said The Gawgon, when I explained what I was doing. "Next time, burn the tip with a match. Now, copy down that poem as I read it out."

The glass inkwell—a pleasant surprise—held nothing but ink, unlike those set into the desks of Rittenhouse Academy, usually jammed with chewing gum, spitballs, dead flies, and un-recognizable foreign objects. I scratched away as The Gawgon dictated fairly rapidly. Finished, I handed over the sheet of paper.

"Almost legible. We'll work on that." The Gawgon leaned her head against the back of the rocking chair. "Enough for today."

Glad to get off so easily, I collected my things. I had started for the door when The Gawgon called me back. She took something from her lap.

"This is for you." She handed me a large hank of yarn as tangled as Dr. McKelvie's beard, knotted, twisted in such a con-fusing mess I could see neither the beginning nor the end of it.

"Take it home," The Gawgon said. "Untie the knots, un-ravel it—as much as you can. Bring it next time."

6

Percy-Us and The Gawgon

f all I had to do was scribble down a few lines of poetry and untie some knots, I reckoned The Gawgon and I might get along very well indeed. To forestall my parents finding someone who would actually make me work, I gave my mother an enthusiastic account of my lesson. When my father came home, I had to describe it to him all over again, including the tangled yarn.

"Chuh! Lawmigawd!" My father lapsed into a Jamaican accent whenever he found Philadelphia English not expressive enough. "Knots? When I was your age, I had to study Euclid."

Sitting in the living room after dinner, I overheard him say to my mother, "If you ask me, old Annie's gone 'round the bend."

"Oh, Alan"—my mother usually began her comments with

"Oh, Alan"—"you shouldn't say things like that. Let her do what she wants, for now."

"But we're paying to have him educated," my father protested.

"I told you there's nothing to pay," my mother said. "I offered, she wouldn't hear of it. No matter how much I insisted. You know how she is when her mind's made up. Too bad. Dear soul, she certainly could have used a little money. She's poor as a church mouse."

Satisfied at the financial arrangement, which amounted to zero, my father went back to the stock-market pages of the newspaper, which he studied as intensely as Uncle Eustace studied the death notices.

Sprawled on my bed, I picked at the knots as The Gawgon ordered. My sister had been entertaining the Tulip Garden. When they disbanded, of course she had to come and poke her nose into my occupation.

"If you were a clever blighter, you'd just take a pair of scissors and cut them," she said, watching me struggle. "Like somebody, whoever it was." My sister was more devoted to her toenails than to classical antiquity.

"Alexander the Great and the Gordian knot," I said. "I read how he chopped it with a sword. I'm not supposed to do that."

My sister soon got bored and left me with the tangled skein. At first, I thought it would be easy, but the knots were tight, the strands twisted every which way. I undid only a couple of them; then I, too, got bored and, grumbling about The Gawgon, tossed the whole thing aside.

Lacking anything better to do, I rummaged out the paint box and amused myself making colored pictures. The details about the hero Perseus were dim in my mind and as complicated as my knotted yarn. I found an easy solution: I ignored most of them.

PERCY-US AND THE TULIP GARDEN

*P*ercy-Us was sitting on a boulder, gloomily polishing his shield, when along came a young man wearing a cap with wings on it, and another pair of wings on the heels of his sandals. He carried a stick with a couple of snakes coiled around it, and still more wings at the tip.

"I am Hermes," he announced, "messenger of the gods."

Even Percy-Us, not the smartest hero in the world, recognized Hermes. Who else dressed like that? "You've got a message for me?"

"Not exactly," said Hermes. "I happened to be passing by. You look like you need cheering up."

"I do," said Percy-Us. "King Polly Deck-Tease is getting married. He's mean, murderous, with Vaseline in his hair. Who'd want to marry him? But that's beside the point. I'm invited to the feast. There's where the trouble comes in. I have to bring a wedding present."

"Napkin rings?" suggested Hermes. "A king always needs napkin rings. State banquets and such. Solid gold is very elegant. I can put in a word with King Midas. He's got plenty. In fact, everything he has is gold. He'll sell cheap."

"I already told the king what I'd give him. I promised"— Percy-Us looked all the more unhappy—"I promised him the head of The Gawgon."

"You what?" cried Hermes. "Fool! Why, for Zeus' sake, did you do a stupid thing like that?"

"I don't know what came over me." Percy-Us sighed. "We were sitting around in the king's hall, his warriors bragging about the gifts they'd bring, all better than any I had. I couldn't stand it. I had to think of something really amazing.

"So, it just popped out," Percy-Us went on. "I swore in front of the king and everybody I'd give him The Gawgon's head. It seemed like a good idea at the time. I'd be a great hero—"

"The first thing about being a great hero," put in Hermes, "is knowing when to keep your mouth shut."

"Too late now," said Percy-Us. "If I fail"—he shuddered— "you can't imagine what he'll do to me."

"Yes, I can," said Hermes. "I don't envy you, my lad. All right. Here, take this sword." He produced a blade from his cloak and handed it to Percy-Us. "You'll need it."

"Call that a sword?" Percy-Us stared in dismay. "It's bent. It looks like a sickle."

"Of course it's bent," said Hermes. "It's a Gawgon-hooker.

By the way," he added, "make sure you never look at The Gawgon. You'll turn to stone. Now listen carefully. You'll need a few more things I don't have with me."

Percy-Us only grew more downcast as Hermes explained what had to be done.

"Good-bye," said Hermes after he finished. "Oh—keep polishing that shield."

Following the directions Hermes gave him, Percy-Us set off. At the end of many days of trudging along twisting pathways, floundering across rivers, and clambering over craggy mountains, he came to a forest grove. There, as Hermes had foretold, he saw a circle of long-stemmed flowers: the sacred Tulip Garden.

It was guarded by beautiful nymphs. As soon as they caught sight of him, they began screaming, shrieking, throwing gravel, and making unfriendly gestures.

"Go away, silly blighter!" yelled Elysia, the head nymph.

"I only want to borrow some of your treasures," protested Percy-Us, "to help me cut off The Gawgon's head."

"We're busy. Can't you see we're painting our toenails?" retorted Elysia. "Get out of here."

"No," declared Percy-Us, despite the nymphs all squealing enough to burst his eardrums. "Give me what I ask or I'll sit here until you do."

"I think he means it," said one of the nymphs as Percy-Us squatted down on a mossy hillock, folded his arms, and showed no sign of moving from the spot.

After a whispered conversation with her sister nymphs, Elysia came up to Percy-Us. She carried several objects.

"Here," she said, handing him a leather bag. "You can stuff The Gawgon's head in it. And here's a pair of sandals."

"I have sandals already."

"Not like these. Strap them on and you can fly through the air whenever you want.

"And this cap . . ." She held up a leather headpiece with long earflaps. "Wear it and you'll be totally invisible."

Percy-Us heartily thanked Elysia and the nymphs and promised to return the items once he finished with them.

"Never mind," said Elysia. "Just go away. Put on that cap. We don't want to see any more of you."

———

The Gawgon seemed a lot brighter than she was after Dr. McKelvie's visit. She had stacked up several books on my card table. When I came in, she was at the rolltop desk picking through some papers. She motioned for me to sit down.

"Show me what you've done with those knots," she said, without further ceremony, and took her place in the rocking chair.

Suddenly wishing I had worked harder at them, I held up the yarn. It looked, if anything, worse than when she gave it to me. The Gawgon snorted something like "Phrumph."

At Rittenhouse Academy, we spent each class period on a separate subject. As I would come to understand, The Gawgon's method—if method it was—mixed everything together, as much a hodgepodge as the knotted yarn. That afternoon, for no particular reason, she had me do arithmetic, which started her talking about Euclid, who invented geometry.

"Do you know geometry? The value of pi?" said The Gawgon. "If you don't, you should."

When I explained that was for Upper School, The Gawgon made another snorting noise. "What nonsense. Why lose time? I have none to waste. Nor do you, for that matter. You have a brain, don't you? You're the paragon of animals."

"The what?" My aforementioned brain, by then, was going in circles.

"William Shakespeare," she went on. "While we're at it, write this down:

"What a piece of work is a man! how noble in reason! how infinite in faculty! in form and moving how express and admirable! in action how like an angel! in apprehension how like a god! the beauty of the world! the paragon of animals! . . .

"As for that," she said, "Captain Jack might hold a different opinion.

"It's from a play called *Hamlet,*" she added. "Bloody, violent, brutal"—she saw she had caught my attention—"so all the more reason to read it, would you say? Apart from being the best play ever written."

She glanced at the little round watch pinned to her black bodice, a signal for me to leave. "Time goes quickly. For me, if not for you."

"It does," I sincerely admitted. "Quicker than school. Really, Gawgon—"

The word was out of my mouth before I realized I had spoken it. No way could I get it back; it seemed to hang in the air, floating in huge capital letters tormentingly beyond reach.

The Gawgon stiffened in the rocking chair and raised an eyebrow. "What was it you said?"

I expected to be turned to stone even as I sat there. I mumbled, "Gawgon."

"I suppose you mean 'Gorgon.' Where did you lick that up?"

I stammered that I must have heard it somewhere from somebody.

"Rosie, no doubt. It sounds like her. That's how you think of me? Next, I daresay you'll want to cut off my head."

I had never hurt an adult's feelings, never, in fact, imagined it was possible that adults had feelings to be hurt. I did not know how to apologize or beg forgiveness. I hung my own head, wishing it had been cut off before I had made such a blunder.

From the corner of my eye I saw her shoulders trembling. I feared she had burst into tears, which would have been still more unbearable, and I was ready to do the same.

She was rocking with laughter.

"Gawgon?" she said, catching her breath. "That's a good reputation to have. Better a Gawgon than a silly old goose. I like it. I like it very much. From now on, that's what you shall call me."

She raised a finger. "But only in private between the two of us. We can enjoy our small secret."

I recovered enough to grin, and asked if I, too, could have a special name.

"Very well," said The Gawgon. "I shall call you—Boy. *The Boy*. With capital initials. The capitals make all the difference."

Happy with that, I got up to leave and started to hand back the yarn.

"Keep it," ordered The Gawgon. "You could stand to learn a little patience and perseverance. If you think those knots are hard, they're nothing compared with the kind you'll have when you're older. Those you'll be untangling for the rest of your life."

The Gawgon pointed to a bowl on the desk. "Take a gumdrop. I recommend the licorice."

7

Captain Jack

The Saturday of my promised overnight visit turned out
to be more of a treat than I expected. Yet another aunt
and uncle had stopped by the boardinghouse. I did not see
them often; they were always very busy, but I adored them
nonetheless.

Aunt Florry, my mother's younger sister, worked as a paid
companion for a Mrs. Heberton, who owned a big estate on
the Main Line. To measure up to the elegance of her surroundings, Aunt Florry had to spend a good bit of her salary on
clothes, and we all admired her for being a nifty dresser. When
I saw her that day, she looked fashionable indeed, trim and neat
in a white linen suit, a Panama hat with a red feather in the
band.

Nifty dresser though she was, I always thought of her as my

dancing aunt. She especially loved the Charleston and tried to teach me the steps. I had difficulty knocking my knees together and wiggling my legs, and she finally gave up. Still, it was a delight to see Aunt Florry in motion.

Along with her came Uncle Will, my mother's youngest brother. He worked for the same Mrs. Heberton as chauffeur and gardener. To me, he was my handsome uncle. I had, on occasion, seen him in his stiff cap with a shiny visor, leather gaiters, and gray tunic, like a dashing cavalry officer. With his wavy black hair and ruddy cheeks, he was the idol of the family. Making him still more romantic, he had a secret sorrow.

"The way that woman treated him absolutely broke his heart," I once heard my grandmother remark to my mother. "I'm not one to go against the law—Prohibition and all that— but I make allowances. Do you wonder the poor boy takes a drop of something now and again?"

On that Saturday, Uncle Will wore civilian clothes, which took nothing away from his air of gallantry. From time to time, he would briefly vanish into the storage shed at the rear of the kitchen and reappear bright-eyed and high-spirited. When my grandmother and Aunt Florry finished making dinner, I took up a tray to Captain Jack's room. His gramophone was going full tilt, playing one of the opera arias he dearly loved, and he did not answer my knock. Obeying standing orders, I left his tray on the floor.

The Gawgon, by then, had come downstairs to the dining room. She gave me an almost imperceptible wink, our secret unspoken and delicious. The Gawgon, like all of us in the sunshine of Uncle Will's presence, was in a fine mood, even joined in a game of Parcheesi—and won.

At the end of the evening came the ceremonial winding of the cuckoo clock, and we trooped into the parlor. The cuckoo lived behind the door of a Swiss chalet carved all in curlicues. To keep the clockwork mechanism going, large iron pinecones hung at the ends of two long chains. It was my honor and privilege to pull them up.

Uncle Will cheered me on as if the pinecones weighed a ton apiece:

"Heave-ho, Skeezix!" he called out. "Hoist the topsail! Haul away, splice the main brace! Steady as she goes!"

Aunt Florry laughed; my grandmother told him, "Oh, Will, you are a caution."

When I finished—making the operation look as strenuous as possible—Uncle Will clapped me on the shoulder.

"Good work, Skeezix," he said. "That should get us through another day."

We waited for the big hand to reach twelve. The door flew open, the cuckoo appeared before its admiring audience, cuckooed the time, then popped back into its cottage and the door snapped shut; all in all, a dramatic event.

Nora, not to be outdone by a mechanical bird, did cuckoo imitations and never let up until I draped a cloth over her cage.

The Gawgon retired. Uncle Will left soon after, saying something vague about an important engagement. The boardinghouse was like an accordion, expanding and contracting according to the number of residents. Now, with lodgers occupying the other bedrooms, the accordion was stretched to its limit, so Aunt Florry doubled up with my grandmother. I was assigned to an old army cot, unfolded and set in a corner of the dining room. I lay full-length on the musty-smelling canvas sling. The cuckoo diligently announced the hours until I lost track of them and my thoughts turned to Percy-Us. I had originally planned to have him cut off The Gawgon's head. But I had grown too fond of The Gawgon herself to allow such a fate, so I relented and made some adjustments.

PERCY-US BRINGS THE GAWGON'S HEAD

*P*ercy-Us put on the cap and sandals the nymphs of the Tulip Garden had given him. Next thing he knew, he was high in the air—a thrilling sensation, except he was flying upside down and backward. Kicking his heels and flapping his arms, it took him some time to get the knack of soaring through the clouds as if he were belly-flopping on a sled.

Since the cap made him invisible, flocks of birds kept bumping into him until he finally took it off.

Soon, Percy-Us saw the mountain range that Hermes had described and swooped down to land at the mouth of a cave, where The Gawgon sat in a rocking chair.

"I've been expecting you, Percy-Us," said The Gawgon. The serpents that covered her head instead of hair had been snoozing; but now they perked up, darted out forked tongues, and fixed him with beady eyes.

Percy-Us made sure not to gaze directly at The Gawgon. Following the advice of Hermes, he used his polished shield as a mirror.

"Speak up. I can't hear you," said The Gawgon. "Stop mumbling into that shield. When you talk to people, it's polite to look at them. Don't you know anything at all about being a hero?"

Percy-Us, too clever to be caught in such a trap, only tightened his grip on the sword. The Gawgon kept on calmly rocking.

"I assume you're here to cut my head off," The Gawgon said. "Very well, get on with it."

Holding up his shield, observing The Gawgon in its reflection, Percy-Us walked backward to her. When he was close enough, he swung his sword in a great, glittering sweep.

Percy-Us miscalculated. He had forgotten that everything reflected in a mirror was reversed. Instead of smiting The Gawgon, he nearly sliced off his own ear.

"Try again," The Gawgon suggested.

Percy-Us made another swipe with his sword, but eyes on the polished shield, he still got mixed up over which was left and which was right. He kept swinging at empty air until he was out of breath.

"This is getting tiresome," said The Gawgon, who kept on rocking while Percy-Us slashed around in all the wrong directions. "You'll do better if you can see what you're trying to chop off.

"Put down that shield and go straight about your business. Don't worry," she added, "you won't be turned to stone. I'll give you something to make you immune."

The Gawgon tossed Percy-Us a licorice gumdrop. "Here, eat this," she said as Percy-Us eyed it distrustfully. "Go on, it will protect you. Gawgons never lie."

Percy-Us chewed up the gumdrop and took a quick peek at The Gawgon. He was glad to find he had not turned to stone.

"That should make things easier," The Gawgon said. "But, before you start chopping, let me review the situation. You need a present for a wedding you don't want to go to, for a king you don't like to begin with. So you blurt out the first thing that comes into your head and promise something you know perfectly well you can't deliver.

"Furthermore"—The Gawgon sharply eyed Percy-Us, who shuffled his feet uncomfortably—"what you promised was at the expense of an innocent bystander who never did you any harm. All for the sake of saving yourself embarrassment, making yourself a hero, and gaining the good opinion of that oaf Polly Deck-Tease. Am I correct so far?"

Percy-Us sheepishly admitted she was.

"That strikes me as utterly selfish," The Gawgon said, "with no regard for anyone's feelings but your own. Stupid, into the bargain. What do you say to that?"

Percy-Us stuttered and stammered and came up with no answer. He finally admitted The Gawgon was right.

"Good," said The Gawgon. "Now you're beginning to think straight even if you can't smite straight. Nevertheless, I recognize you've gone to some effort. That's commendable; I give you credit. So, I'll tell you what I'm going to do."

The Gawgon explained her plan, to which Percy-Us heartily agreed. Hand in hand with The Gawgon, he soared into the air, and the two of them flew quickly to the palace of King Polly Deck-Tease.

While The Gawgon waited outside the door, Percy-Us strode into the great hall. The bride had not yet arrived, but the impatient Polly Deck-Tease and his warriors had already started feasting and reveling, gobbling refreshments by the handful.

"Aha!" shouted Polly Deck-Tease. "There you are! About time. You brought me The Gawgon's head?"

"Yes," Percy-Us replied, "I certainly did."

"Let's have it, then," Polly Deck-Tease ordered. "So far, my only wedding presents are a lot of napkin rings."

Percy-Us tossed him the leather sack. Sucking his teeth in gleeful anticipation, Polly Deck-Tease opened it. His jaw dropped.

"Empty!" he burst out. "Nothing! What kind of joke is this? You broke your promise, you boasting, bragging, pathetic excuse for a hero! I don't like being disappointed, especially on my wedding day. You'll regret trifling with me. I'll have you diced up and deep-fried in boiling oil."

"I didn't break my promise," Percy-Us replied. "I told you I'd bring The Gawgon's head. So I did."

Having put on the cap of invisibility, The Gawgon stepped into the hall.

"And all the rest of her, too," said Percy-Us.

The Gawgon took off the cap and glared at the revelers. Instantly, they turned to stone. Polly Deck-Tease, shaking a fist, stood literally petrified. Some of the warriors had stayed seated, others climbed to their feet, still others held goblets in upraised hands, motionless as marble statues.

"Nice garden ornaments," The Gawgon said. "Someday, no doubt, they'll be in the British Museum."

Percy-Us, delighted everything had ended so well, flew The Gawgon to her cave, thanked her, and was about to leave when he stopped and turned back.

"For a Gawgon," he said, "you're not a bad sort."

"For a hero," said The Gawgon, "you're not a bad sort either."

━━━━━━━━━━━━━ **Thuh End** ━━━━━━━━━━━━━

Sunday morning, Uncle Will had not come back; no one had heard anything from him. The rest of us ate the traditional Sunday pancakes. After stuffing myself, I carried a breakfast tray to Captain Jack's room.

His dinner, untouched, was on the floor where I had left it the night before. I feared his breakfast might suffer the same fate, but when I knocked, he called me in.

A nose-prickling haze of Turkish tobacco smoke hung in

the air. The canvas window shade had been pulled down to the sill; sunlight filtered through it in a yellowish glow. A bare bulb, unlit, hung from the end of an electric cord in the middle of the ceiling. Captain Jack's bed was rumpled, the bolster and half the covers on the floor. The most prominent piece of furniture was his gramophone: a tall cabinet with a hinged lid, and on one side, a handle to crank the mechanism. Captain Jack himself, unshaven, still in his BVDs, sprawled in an armchair. He grinned at me and gave a loose kind of salute:

"First Sergeant. Report."

"Company all present and accounted for, sir." I straightened to attention, then marched forward to set the tray on his lap.

Captain Jack picked up the tin shaped like a log cabin and watched the syrup pour out. It seemed to fascinate him.

"Been on the sick list, I hear," he said at last. "Returned to duty? Good. And that bloody bird strong as ever?"

I assured him Nora was fine.

Captain Jack grimaced. "She ought to be roasted for Christmas. She'll drive me 'round the bend with her bloody screeching."

I felt sorry Captain Jack hated Nora, but let it go. My grandmother always told me never to worry over anything Captain Jack said or did; he had his good days and bad. Now, though he had drenched his pancakes with syrup, he only picked at them.

I mentioned that Aunt Annie—I almost said "Gawgon"—

was giving me lessons. I told him she recited something about man being the paragon of animals and that he might have a different opinion.

"Paragon?" Captain Jack said. "Not the ones I've seen. Not in the trenches. Only animals. Live like pigs, die like pigs. There's your paragon."

It sounded gruesome but interesting. I asked him to tell me more about the Great War.

"The war to end all wars?" Captain Jack said. "It's loud, it's dirty, and it stinks. Horses scream worse than anybody when they're hit. Over and done with now. Just thank God you'll never have to go through anything like it."

Captain Jack was staring past me into the distance. I asked him if he wanted to play some records.

"Eh?" He focused on me again. He knew I loved to crank up the gramophone and open its wooden shutters, like venetian blinds, to make it louder. "Whatever you please, First Sergeant."

He enjoyed his operas, so I put the quartet from *Rigoletto* on the turntable, carefully lowering the arm with its steel needle onto the first groove. Captain Jack settled into his chair and shut his eyes. For variety, I put on a comic song we listened to occasionally, very bright and jolly. A man's voice came through the shutters; it sounded as if he were singing from the bottom of a bucket with a tinny brass accompaniment.

"Keep your head down, Fritzie boy," he taunted, while the trombone brayed impudently:

Keep your head down, Fritzie boy.
Late last night in the pale moonlight,
I saw you, I saw you.
You were fixing your barbed wire
When we opened rapid fire.
If you want to see your father
In the Fatherland,
Keep your head down, Fritzie boy.

"Enough of that," Captain Jack snapped. "Not in the mood for it."

I hurried to lift the needle before the band started a second chorus.

"It's true, you know," he said, less harshly. "Moonlight— almost bright as day. You can see a man's face at a hundred yards."

He held out the tray. "Bloody song soured my stomach. Take this away. You're a good boy, First Sergeant. Dismissed."

I closed the door behind me. Captain Jack had put on *Tosca* and was singing along with the tenor. In the parlor, Nora was hanging upside down from the top of her cage and, as if taking revenge on Captain Jack for his remarks, screeching her head off.

8

The Gawgon and the Sphinx

he nose of the Sphinx is missing," said The Gawgon.
"Most of it. Blame that on the Emperor Napoleon—no,
not yet emperor then. Only General Bonaparte."

"Bones-Apart," I said.

"Sometimes, Boy," said The Gawgon, "you can be very silly.
Well, in any event, he let his troops use it for target practice. A
pudgy little man, Napoleon, with that spit curl on his forehead
and a hand in his jacket as if he had to scratch. Small, for an
emperor."

The Gawgon had been following her custom of exploring
odd byways, more exciting than my plodding classes at Rittenhouse Academy. That afternoon, she had started me on pen-
manship exercises to improve my deplorable handwriting.

"The trick is in the wrist," The Gawgon said. "You'll get

the hang of it. Be glad you don't have to write in Egyptian hieroglyphics."

That had set her off on a detour to ancient Egypt. The Sphinx and Napoleon wandered in, along with statuary and wall carvings.

"The old pharaohs built things to last," The Gawgon said. "Temples, pyramids—still standing, mostly. A little the worse for wear; impressive, nonetheless. I'll never forget the first time I saw them."

"You were there?" I never imagined The Gawgon being anywhere but in her room.

"Long ago. A couple and their young daughter were touring Egypt, Greece, Italy. They hired me as a governess." The Gawgon smiled. "Governess? I was hardly more than a girl myself."

I could believe The Gawgon was ancient enough to have seen the Pyramids under construction. But—a girl? Never.

"Oh, yes," The Gawgon said, as if reading my thoughts. "Does that surprise you?"

She went to a pigeonhole in the rolltop desk and sorted through a packet of papers. "There was another Philadelphian in that gaggle of tourists. A young fellow who thought himself quite the photographer."

The Gawgon handed me a fragile picture. "He took this of me on the pyramid of Cheops. I wanted to climb to the top, but everyone kept shouting at me to come down, afraid I'd break my neck. Scandalized, more likely. I had on riding breeches, shocking for a female."

I peered at the photo, wafer-thin and brittle. Yet the image was sharp. Perched on a block of stone halfway up the sloping wall, a beautiful, bright-eyed girl gazed straight at the camera, grinning all over her face. I did not recognize The Gawgon at first. I glanced at her. The girl's features showed faintly behind The Gawgon's, like the lines of a drawing badly erased.

"When the photograph was ready," The Gawgon continued, "he made a great show of presenting it to me in front of all the other tourists. 'For the intrepid lady explorer,' he said. 'As fair as she is fearless.' He was a cheeky rascal—but I was the one who got scolded. My employers said I'd been flirtatious." The Gawgon chuckled. "Perhaps they were right.

"I never did see inside the tombs. Most were empty, anyway, ransacked by grave robbers. A fellow named Howard Carter found the biggest treasure a few years ago. Marvelous things. He dug into the burial chamber of Tutankhamen, a boy king about your age. 'King Tut,' the newspapers called him."

We had gone well past our time. Instead of my mother driving me, I was able to walk home by myself. So, I would have stayed longer, but looking wan, The Gawgon dismissed me.

"You've hardly touched those knots, Boy," she said.

Exactly when, I could not be sure, but it was during one of those summer afternoons that The Gawgon captured my total devotion and allegiance. Because she saw me for whatever I was. No longer the Amazing Invisible Boy, with her I had noth-

ing to hide. She made me feel my mind was free to do as it
pleased. A mystery of the heart? I could not solve it, nor did I
care to.

In any case, I came to imagine her as mistress of time and
space, expert in all disguises, who went wherever she chose, did
whatever she chose, knew all that was to be known. To me, she
was capable of everything and anything.

For the simple reason, no further explanation required, she
was: The Gawgon.

THE GAWGON AND NAPOLEON
BONES-APART

*U*nbeknownst to the Turkish overlords of Egypt, unsuspected
by the authorities in Cairo, The Gawgon and I had set up head-
quarters underground between the paws of the Sphinx.

The Gawgon, convinced that most of this colossal statue lay
beneath the desert sands, thought it would be interesting to explore what she suspected was a maze of chambers and galleries
untouched for thousands of years.

We had hired a pair of expert grave robbers and highly
competent ransackers to do the digging and heavy lifting; their
loyalty and devotion were assured by generous cash payments
from The Gawgon's unlimited financial resources. While Mustafa and Ali stood awaiting instructions, The Gawgon bent over
a folding table and, by the glow of an oil lamp, sketched out a
plan. For the occasion, she wore a French army officer's uni-

form and disguised herself as a young girl, her long red-gold hair tied with a tricolor ribbon.

"There is a logic in architecture, Boy, as in everything else," she said. "If a chamber is—here, logically a passage should be—here."

The Gawgon stopped. Her keen ears had detected noises aboveground. A moment later, I myself heard them: a series of crackling explosions like a string of firecrackers on the Fourth of July—although the Egyptians did not celebrate our glorious national holiday.

We cautiously made our way up to the desert floor. Some yards distant, a regiment of French infantrymen lounged about, tunics unbuttoned, cocked hats askew. Some were drinking from wine bottles or playing cards on drumheads; others were firing their muskets at the Sphinx. Half the nose had already been shot away; another volley sent chips of stone raining on our heads.

"Halt, you idiots!" cried The Gawgon. "*Cessez* and *désistez* immediately!"

Dumbfounded to see a beautiful young girl in military garb snapping orders at them, the soldiers gaped and lowered their muskets. The Gawgon strode up and began tongue-lashing them for being worse than their ancestors, the barbarian Gauls. The shamefaced troops hung their heads. An angry figure came stamping through the ranks.

"*Parbleu!* A thousand thunders! What is it that this is?"

The pudgy little man wore a blue jacket dripping with gold

braid, epaulets thick as hairbrushes; in his cocked hat, a blue, white, and red rosette; plastered on his perspiring brow, a curl like an upside-down question mark. He thrust his jaw at The Gawgon, who calmly observed him.

"How dare you to overrule my authority, monsieur?" he cried. "But—but a thousand pardons, I mistake myself. It is a most fetching mademoiselle!" He reached out and tweaked The Gawgon's ear. "Who is it that you are?"

"This is Le Garçon—The Boy." The Gawgon, reclaiming her ear, indicated me. "And, General Bonaparte, I am: The Gawgon."

"La Gaugonne!" Napoleon caught his breath. "Le Garçon! I have heard of your astonishing capabilities. Your fame precedes you. Do me the honor of joining me for a glass of champagne in my tent."

"We aren't thirsty," said The Gawgon. "The Boy and I have other things to do. As for yourself, General, allowing your troops to vandalize the treasures of antiquity, you should be ashamed."

"*Moi?* What will you of me?" Napoleon shrugged his shoulders and spread his hands in that exasperating gesture the French have so perfected. "It is but an old and badly damaged Sphinx. The Turks, the Arabs, all the world shoots at it. How else to pass the time in this abominable desert?" He stopped to insert a hand between the buttons of his waistcoat. "*Pardonnez.* Ah, these accursed sand fleas! They attack me in battalions without mercy. And, as well, my digestion suffers in this heat.

"Mademoiselle, we do not vandalize"—he scratched awhile longer—"we preserve. Accompany yourself with me. I shall demonstrate."

We followed Napoleon to the rear of the encampment. He pulled away a canvas cover and proudly pointed at a heap of objects: statuettes, golden bowls, elaborately painted jars, a mummy case with a reclining figure carved on the lid.

"Voilà!" he declared. "I am rescuing these from the unworthy hands of the enemy. They will be safely transported, now that I have captured Egypt for La Belle France."

"Captured?" retorted The Gawgon. "Who captured who? Let me say two words: Royal Navy."

Napoleon's face went pale as Camembert cheese. The Gawgon pressed on:

"At Abukir Bay, the British fleet devastated you. Even now, you are blockaded, bottled up, your Egyptian campaign a disaster."

"A small setback," protested Napoleon. "It shall be rectified."

"I doubt that," said The Gawgon. "Your government feared you were getting too big for your breeches—so to speak. They secretly wished to see you defeated, your reputation ruined. They sent you to Egypt, certain you would fail miserably. As indeed you have done."

"Those swine! Those cows!" burst out Napoleon. "I shall foil their treacherous plot and revenge myself on them. I remain in Egypt until victory."

"That could be a long time," said The Gawgon. "Meanwhile—I do not repeat gossip and tittle-tattle, but there has been talk of the beautiful Madame Bonaparte and certain handsome young officers."

"Joséphine! *Diable!*" Napoleon's cheeks went plum-colored. "No sooner do I turn my back than she cavorts herself!"

He shouted for his adjutant, gave him command of the army, and ordered him to make the best of a bad situation. "I depart to Paris immediately!"

"You can't escape, General," I warned. "The British blockade—"

"A fig for perfidious Albion! A nation of shopkeepers! I must keep the eye on that charming but naughty Joséphine. I shall hire a sardine boat, a felucca, a raft if necessary."

An orderly led up a prancing white horse. Without another word, Napoleon leaped astride and galloped off in a whirlwind of sand.

The regiment hurriedly broke camp, tossing away knapsacks, blanket rolls, and other gear that would slow their hasty withdrawal. Even the pile of looted treasure was abandoned.

As Mustafa and Ali joined us, The Gawgon went to examine the objects. "If I read the hieroglyphics correctly, this sarcophagus holds the remains of young King Tut."

"Where did it come from?" I asked. "We have to hide it safely. These other things, too. We can't just leave them lying around in the desert."

The Gawgon turned to Mustafa and Ali. "Take it to the Valley of the Kings. Find an empty tomb and haul everything into it. After that, wall it up so no one will suspect the chamber exists."

She fixed an eye on our attendant grave robbers. "Listen, you two. If you breathe a word of this, if you so much as think about sneaking back and rifling the tomb, I promise I'll hound you into your graves and make mummies of you."

The Gawgon's threat, accompanied by handfuls of gold coins, so deeply touched the hearts of Mustafa and Ali that they salaamed, groveled, and swore every oath to seal their lips for eternity.

"Nothing like terror and bribery to encourage good moral conduct," The Gawgon remarked as we set about loading King Tut and his trove onto our camels. "I'm confident those bazaar ruffians will keep their mouths shut. I'm also confident some reasonably intelligent person will, in time, find these treasures and treat them with proper respect."

The Gawgon smiled at the Sphinx looming in front of us. "There's someone, at least, who'll never tell our secret."

The Sphinx smiled back at her.

9

The Gawgon Walks Abroad

In late summer, Mr. Digby, one of my father's Jamaican chums, stopped off during a business trip. Looking very tropical in a cream-colored suit, a planter's straw hat, and a bristly mustache, he was installed with great excitement in our spare room. To make a grand occasion, my mother cooked a dinner featuring rice and peas, mangoes, fried plantains, and other delicacies.

Aunt Marta and Uncle Eustace were, of course, invited. He, my father, and Mr. Digby had not seen each other for some while. Suddenly they were all boys again, laughing like mad, drifting into Jamaican dialect, calling each other by their old nicknames: "Mackerel Fat" for Uncle Eustace, "Dog Flea" for my father, and, for Mr. Digby, "Diggers."

After dinner, Diggers brought down a glass jar from his

suitcase. The object of his trip, he explained, was to recruit salesmen for a miraculous new product.

"Palm-Nutto," Diggers declared. "It cleans. It scrubs. Anything, everything. Carpets, pots and pans—you can do the laundry or wash your face with it." At this, he unscrewed the jar and fingered out a dollop of yellowish paste.

"Completely harmless," he said, gulping down the Palm-Nutto. "Good for the bowels, too."

My father and Uncle Eustace declined this chance at a fortune. Palm-Nutto did not fit in with Oriental goods or tombstones, and Diggers dropped the subject.

My mother proposed driving to Atlantic City next day. Uncle Eustace had an appointment with a grieving widow, but the rest of us thought it was a wonderful idea.

Then I realized next day was my Friday lesson. On the one hand, I loved the seashore, amusement piers, splashing in the surf, and an opportunity to pee in the Atlantic Ocean. Irresistible charms. On the other hand, The Gawgon had taken me to Moscow, Napoleon's disastrous retreat through howling Russian blizzards, and left me deliciously agonized in suspense when he was exiled to a rocky island. I knew, from school, that he was defeated at the Battle of Waterloo. But The Gawgon had some magical way of turning mind-numbing history into new adventures, equally irresistible.

When I explained my difficulty to my mother, she simply said the choice was mine. My sister, surprisingly, came out in favor of Atlantic City. And that was what tipped the balance.

"Give Aunt Annie a rest," she said. "She's had to put up with you all week. She'll be glad to get rid of you for a day."

"She won't be glad," I flung back angrily. "She won't be glad at all. Neither will I."

I decided to stay with The Gawgon.

THE GAWGON AND MAMMA LETIZIA

We were relaxing on the terrace of The Gawgon's villa on the Riviera. For the time being, she had assumed the guise of an older lady of quality, certainly very rich. We had spent the evening in Monte Carlo, whose elegance and sophistication were matched only by Atlantic City's. In the glittering casino, The Gawgon and I had won so much at roulette that the tearful manager implored us to leave before we broke the bank, and we graciously complied.

One of the servants came to announce a caller who declined to reveal her name. The Gawgon, always curious about unidentified visitors, agreed to receive her. Moments later there arrived a massively stout, elderly woman with swollen ankles and a gold tooth. In voluminous, shiny black skirts, a black shawl over her head, she dropped with difficulty to her knees and begged The Gawgon's help.

"My boy, *mon enfant!*" she wailed in a heavy Corsican accent, more Italian than French. "His enemies have put him on an island. Exiled, forbidden to leave—"

"I take it," broke in The Gawgon, "you are Madame Bona-parte, mother of the ex-emperor."

"Please, call me Mamma Letizia," said Madame Bonaparte. "My Napoleone—I warned him he one day would go too far. Yes, a naughty boy, fighting wars with everybody. But always kind and loving to his mamma. Now his little heart breaks with unhappiness. He will surely die of boredom and misery."

The Gawgon agreed to do all she could, and Mamma Letizia left after showering her with blessings.

"In principle, I'm not fond of emperors," said The Gawgon. "Troublemakers, most of them. Worse than spoiled brats. Napoleon? I haven't decided if he was a good emperor who did some bad things, or a bad emperor who did some good things. But, compared with Louis the Eighteenth, that nincompoop who took his throne, Napoleon looks better and better."

The Gawgon quickly dispatched a number of secret messages and made other preparations. Within a matter of days, we were aboard a fishing boat in the Mediterranean, sailing past the tip of Corsica to the tiny isle of Elba.

In the first light of dawn, we made out a figure with a telescope observing us from the shore. The Gawgon instructed the helmsman to make for a sheltered cove. Moments later, we tied up at a rickety pier. Napoleon clambered aboard, and we cast off for the open sea.

Wrapped in a threadbare greatcoat, a sailor's knitted cap on his head, Napoleon did not immediately recognize The Gawgon, who wore a sea cloak and had pasted on a false beard and mustache. When he realized her identity, he was pathetically grateful:

"Ah, La Gaugonne! Angel of mercy to extract me from this shabby, third-rate island! It has been insupportable, *morbleu!*"

"Ordinarily," said The Gawgon, "I prefer to let the high and mighty get themselves out of their own messes. I'm only doing this for your mamma's sake."

"My beloved mamma!" Napoleon clasped his hands. "To see her son brought so low! *Non, non,* that is not just. A thousand devils and *zut, alors!* Why did I sell the Louisiana so cheap? I could have gone there and built a new empire of the Western Hemisphere."

I suggested he might yet reach New Orleans, an easygoing town that asked no questions. He could surely find a job of some sort.

"*Moi?* Do you see me as, what, a sauce maker? A pastry cook?" Napoleon thrust his fingers into his vest. "Impossible! Being emperor spoils one for any other trade."

That instant, cutting through the sea mist, a British warship sped toward us. We were hailed, commanded to heave to, and encouraging us to obey, a cannon blasted a warning shot across our bow.

The Gawgon drew Napoleon aside, whispered quickly, then ordered him and the crew amidships to start cleaning tubs of fish. The captain's longboat, meantime, had come alongside; the captain and half a dozen sailors climbed a rope ladder to our deck.

"Jolly good of you to stop without making us blow you out of the water, haw, haw!" declared the officer. "Got wind of a bit of a plot to spirit away Bony-Party. Deuced inconvenient, sorry, but I'm to search all vessels hereabouts."

"Search away. We have no emperors aboard." The Gawgon's answer was hairsplitting although technically true, since Napoleon had been deposed. "Only a cargo of fish, as you see."

"And smell, too, by Jove!" The captain pulled a scented lace handkerchief from his sleeve and waved it under his nose. He glanced sharply at the crew busily gutting fish, and stepped closer. "Fine lot of villainous rascals, wot? This one especially. You there, let's have a look at you."

It was all The Gawgon and I could do to keep silent as the captain went on:

"Well, you're as scurvy and scrofulous a fellow as I've ever seen. No emperor, that's for sure. Unless you're the emperor of sardines and anchovies, haw, haw!"

The captain added other scornful comments, then gaped as the object of this bullyragging leaped to his feet and began shouting insults in return. The knitted cap fell off the man's head, revealing an unmistakable lovelock on his brow.

"Egad! Good heavens, 'pon my word—Bony himself!" The captain immediately ordered his men to seize the fish-gutter, who roared and cursed furiously. While the sailors shackled their raging captive, the officer strode to The Gawgon, accused her of being part of the conspiracy, and threatened to clap her in irons.

"Why blame me?" The Gawgon innocently replied. "I use whatever crew I can hire, no telling who they are. You know how difficult it is to get help these days."

"All too true." The captain sighed. "Can't even find a decent butler. What terrible times we live in! Well, then, sail on about your business. Pip–pip, cheerio."

When the warship was out of sight, The Gawgon whistled through her teeth. From his hiding place in the hold, soaking wet and reeking of fish, climbed Napoleon.

"An impostor to take my place! A ruse worthy of myself!" he cried. "Those fools will ship him back to Elba before they realize he is not me!"

"Thank your mamma," said The Gawgon. "I asked her to find someone to pass for you. In case of emergency, it's always good to have a spare emperor."

"A perfect resemblance," I said to The Gawgon as Napoleon strutted up and down the deck, "but I was worried when he started yelling at the captain. He wasn't speaking French, he was speaking Italian."

"The British can't tell the difference," The Gawgon said. "If it isn't English, it's all Greek to them."

The Mediterranean turned choppy; a contrary wind kept us from making rapid headway. But, at last, we sighted the French coast and climbed into the boat's dinghy. The Gawgon and I rowed for shore while Napoleon stood in the bow congratulating himself and scoffing at the English for being such dupes. Too impatient for us to beach our little craft, he jumped out and went sloshing through the surf.

"I march to Paris *immédiatement*," declared Napoleon. "My veteran troops, my loyal and adoring people of France will join me along the way. My empire will rise again. *C'est magnifique!*

"I shall put up statues of you both," Napoleon added, "and name our grandest thoroughfares 'Avenue de la Gaugonne' and 'Boulevard du Garçon.'"

"Don't bother," said The Gawgon. "You'll have enough on your mind."

"Do you know a town called Waterloo?" I put in.

"Of course. In Belgium." Napoleon shrugged. "A mere nothing of a place."

"Yes, well," I said, "don't go there."

Thuh End

"I hear you gave up a trip to the seashore," The Gawgon said, next morning. "That surprises me."

My mother had dropped me off at the boardinghouse. Since everyone would be home late, I was to sleep over. I told The Gawgon I didn't want to go to Atlantic City and would rather stay with her.

"I take that as a high compliment," The Gawgon said. "Yes, Boy, I'm very touched.

"But fair is fair," she added, after a few moments. "You gave up one holiday. You'll have another."

The Gawgon got to her feet. "Lessons can wait. Come along, Boy. We're taking a ride."

When I understood what she meant, I still could hardly believe it.

The Gawgon was going out of the house.

10

In the Pale Moonlight

"Annie, do you think it's wise? Do you really think it's sensible?"

My grandmother and The Gawgon were talking quietly in the downstairs hall. A closet had produced a wide-brimmed straw hat and a pair of white gloves long unused, smelling of lavender. The Gawgon skewered the hat to her bun of white hair with the longest hat pin I had ever seen and examined the effect in a mirror. Had she been my sister, I would have called it primping.

"Mary, can you tell me," The Gawgon said, "have I ever been wise? Have I ever been sensible?"

"Dr. McKelvie—" my grandmother began.

"Pshaw!" The Gawgon made a final adjustment. "What

does he know? The boy's given me a new lease on life, which is more than that pill-roller's done."

My grandmother watched us from the parlor window as we crossed the porch and The Gawgon picked her way down the front steps. She had armed herself with a cane from the umbrella stand; an ordinary walking stick, but it would not have surprised me to see her unscrew the handle and snatch out a sword blade.

For the promised ride, I believed The Gawgon capable of summoning a coach and four, maybe a chariot. What she had in mind was: a bus.

We waited on the corner. Double-decker buses ran on Larchmont Street. I loved the upper deck, with the wind whistling, the bus lurching as if about to capsize. When it arrived, I expected her to prefer sitting below, but gripping her cane, The Gawgon climbed the narrow spiral stairway to the heights.

"Excelsior!" cried The Gawgon as we settled ourselves on a wooden bench. "That means 'higher' in Latin."

Ignoring the raised eyebrows of our fellow passengers, she began declaiming:

> The shades of night were falling fast,
> As through an Alpine village pass'd
> A youth, who bore, 'mid snow and ice,
> A banner, with the strange device—
> Excelsior!

"It goes on and on," said The Gawgon. "I've forgotten most of it, which I count as a blessing. I'm sure it had deep meaning for Henry Wadsworth Longfellow; he was always partial to deep meanings. I happen to think it's one of the silliest poems in the English language."

The poem "Excelsior," The Gawgon explained, told of a youth with sad brow and flashing eyes hauling a big flag up the Alps. Everyone warned him against avalanches and raging torrents. A village maiden urged him to stay and rest his head on her breast.

"But no," said The Gawgon, "he kept climbing, holding up his flag, and shouting 'Excelsior!' at every whipstitch. A Saint Bernard found him frozen to death. Now, it's all very commendable trying to reach the heights of anything. But only an idiot would go mountaineering with a flapping big piece of cloth. Nonsense! The fool ended up dead, no use to anyone including himself."

We climbed off the bus at Fifty-second Street and plunged into a delicious stew of pretzel carts, hot-dog stands, cigar stores, crowded sidewalks, and not one but two movie houses. Aunt Rosie complained it was a loud, impolite street with a lot of suspicious riffraff. I thought it was the most exciting place in the world. I was delighted that The Gawgon chose to take me there.

"Off we go to seek our fortune," declared The Gawgon. "To El Dorado, realm of gold."

I had no idea what she meant, which only made it more

mysterious, and, of course, I would have followed her any-where. It took The Gawgon a short while to find a shop just off Fifty-second Street. The only things close to gold were three brass balls hanging over the door.

Before we entered, she swore me to secrecy:

"I could have asked your father to sell my little trinket in his store, but he'd have fussed at me and bought it himself—charitably. This is nobody's business but mine. So, not a word to anyone."

I solemnly swore and we went inside. The Gawgon held up her skirts to keep them off the sticky floor. The place smelled like old mushrooms. Yet it was a kind of El Dorado, jam-packed with guitars, banjos, fiddles, racks of clothing, bins of household goods. The showcase displayed watches, jewelry, and a number of military medals.

From her purse, The Gawgon took a small brooch and mo-tioned me to move back. She stepped up to a heavy-jowled, flinty-eyed man who did not look friendly. Without knowing why, I felt embarrassed for her, and for myself, a little queasy. Their conversation was some sort of business between adults, and I should not be listening. The Gawgon, undaunted, rapped her knuckles on the countertop:

"My dear sir, I'll thank you not to take me for a fool," she said. "The gold alone is worth more than that."

The man grumbled, but under The Gawgon's unwavering eyes, he finally shrugged and took some dollar bills from his cash drawer. The Gawgon handed over the brooch, accepted a receipt, and we left.

"That, Boy, is a pawnshop," The Gawgon said as we headed back to Fifty-second Street. "Not a nice kind of place, but sooner or later, you'll find there's a seamy side of life. It's where poor people borrow money and leave something behind. When they come to repay, they get their property again. Otherwise, the pawnbroker sells it. I don't intend coming back.

"What I do intend," she added, "is spending it all like a drunken sailor."

Of everything I could imagine The Gawgon being, drunken sailor was not one. As for spending, she indeed led us on a daylong spree.

First, we went to the fancier of the two picture palaces. It featured a vaudeville show: a magician, a dancing dog, and spangled ladies kicking up their legs to the boops and yawps of the Wurlitzer organ. I made little sense of the movie that followed: mostly men in tuxedos and women in slippery gowns gazing at each other through drooping eyelids. Nobody got killed or maimed.

"I'd forgotten they talk now," The Gawgon said behind her hand. "More's the pity. There's too much yammering already."

Still, that would have been treat enough in itself. But The Gawgon had more in mind. After the movie, she found a combination bookstore and stationery store. There, she bought some books—their titles were unfamiliar to me, but she assured

me I would like them and we would read them together later.
As well, she bought a deck of cards with letters instead of jacks,
queens, and kings.

"Anagrams," The Gawgon said. "You deal them out and try
to make words."

The spending spree ended when we went to a hot-dog and
orange-juice stand. The Gawgon drew some attention from the
other customers. Seeing her straw hat with its huge pin, her
long black skirts, white gloves, and cane, they probably expected more genteel behavior, but The Gawgon chomped her
hot dog with carefree abandon.

"McKelvie should see me now." The Gawgon had a mis-
chievous glint in her eyes. "Pass the relish, Boy, if you please."

We rode the bus back to Larchmont Street, belching tri-
umphantly in the gathering dusk.

My grandmother was as relieved to see us as if we had been
on a perilous expedition up the Alps or down the Amazon. The
Gawgon went to her room for a nap. I was too excited to rest.
True to my word, I said nothing of the pawnshop, yet alone
with my grandmother, I wanted to ask about something that
lingered, troublesome, in my head.

I had the impression Dr. McKelvie would not have approved of our outing. I was curious to know why. But I did not
ask. The young did not question the mysterious lives of their
elders. Instead, that night, I stretched out on my cot and drifted
away to Switzerland.

THE HEIGHTS OF THE MATTERHORN

*T*he shades of night were falling fast when The Gawgon and I reached a little village high in the Alps. Lamps already glowed cozily; the villagers were snug indoors. The Gawgon, brushing ice pellets from her cloak, stepped through the door of the local inn. I followed, carrying the long staff and its huge banner embroidered with a single word in fancy curlicues: EXCELSIOR.

During our ascent through mountain mist and drizzle, the banner had grown so damp and heavy we were obliged to take turns carrying it. The Gawgon, outfitted like myself in leather breeches and hobnailed boots, coils of rope at our shoulders, ice axes at our belts, called for hot cider. I looked around for some place to park the cumbersome burden and finally leaned it against the serving counter, where it dripped a large puddle of ice water.

"Mein Gott!" The innkeeper paled when The Gawgon told him our destination. "The peak of the Matterhorn? This time of year? Not possible!"

"Possible or not," The Gawgon declared, "The Boy and I have an urgent mission. We must accomplish it at all cost."

As the innkeeper warned against this foolhardy venture, mentioning avalanches, raging torrents, and gaping chasms, his beautiful daughter approached me.

"O youth with flashing eyes," she said winsomely, "what signifies this banner and its strange device? An advertisement for some new product? Breakfast cereal, perhaps, like Swiss muesli?"

At a loss to offer satisfactory explanation, I could only say our task was of utmost importance.

"Ach, nein!" The maiden clasped her hands. "Do not to your doom go! With me here stay and rest." She batted her eyelashes and cast me a sidelong glance. "I will let you my cuckoo clock wind up."

Though tempted, I politely declined. The Gawgon finished her cider and we set off again, climbing ever upward through the night. The peak glinted icily in the pale moonlight, bone-chilling gales swept from the heights. Barely halfway up the slope, The Gawgon halted. Before us yawned a deep crevasse.

"We can't climb down one side and up the other." The Gawgon, chin in hand, made mental calculations. "A little too wide to jump across. Very well, Boy, furl that silly flag. Give it here."

I did as she asked. The Gawgon took the flagstaff and, with perfect precision, tipped it lengthwise across the chasm, where it lay like a bridge—but a bridge no wider than a tightrope.

"No, we won't dance across like acrobats," she said, when I asked if that was her intention. "More like a couple of monkeys."

As she ordered, we flung away our rucksacks and other gear to lighten our weight. The Gawgon then leaped into the crevasse, deftly caught hold of the flagstaff, and hand over hand, swung along its length and heaved herself up on the far edge.

I tried to do likewise, but a frosty film already covered the staff. One hand slipped. I hung, dangling and kicking, until I regained my grasp then swung my way across, never daring to look down until The Gawgon pulled me safely to my feet.

Retrieving the flag, I clambered after The Gawgon, ever higher. Despite the bitter cold, I was drenched with sweat, which quickly froze. I crackled with ice inside and outside my clothing. All that night, we pressed upward. One last assault and we would gain the pinnacle.

Our perils had not ended. Deep rumblings shook the mountainside. Snowdrifts as big as Swiss chalets careened downward. We scurried out of their path as they roared by. But no sooner did we think ourselves safe than a giant snowball hurtled straight at The Gawgon.

She had no time to dodge as it bounced down the slope. Without a moment's thought, summoning all my strength, I flung the flagstaff like a spear.

The tip of the staff struck the sphere on its upward bounce. The impact jarred the titanic snowball off its deadly course, and it landed harmlessly a few feet away. With the flagstaff sticking out of it, it looked like a huge vanilla lollipop.

"Well, Boy, I do believe you saved my life," said The Gawgon as I pulled the staff loose. "I appreciate that. Hurry along now. One avalanche is enough."

Just before daybreak, we made our final ascent. Stars filled the sky, but they began winking out as pink streaks rose above the Alpine range.

A figure stood at the top of the Matterhorn. Wrapped in an overcoat, its collar turned up to his ears, he stamped his feet and beat his arms against his sides. His bushy white beard had frozen stiff. Despite the muffler around his neck and the hat jammed down tight on his head, I recognized him from a portrait I had seen in one of The Gawgon's books.

It was Henry Wadsworth Longfellow.

"What took you so long?" he called out in a peevish voice. He pointed his frozen beard accusingly at us. "I've been waiting all night; I could have caught my death of cold."

"Don't take that tone with me, Henry," retorted The Gawgon. "You asked me to do you a favor, and I did. Here's your flag. Good-bye. The Boy and I are going home."

Without so much as a word of thanks, Longfellow impatiently unfurled the banner. One hand behind his back, the other clutching the staff, he cast his eyes heavenward, lost in solemn contemplation of the vast panorama.

The Gawgon motioned for me to begin the downward climb. I hung back.

"As long as we're here," I said to her, "I want to ask him: Really, what does all this mean? I don't understand the point of it."

"Let him alone," said The Gawgon. "Poets don't like to be questioned, especially when they don't know the answers."

━━━━━━━━━━━━━━ **Thuh End** ━━━━━━━━━━━━━━

Something woke me. I must have been tossing and turning on the cot, the sheets were tangled around my legs. Moonlight shone through the parlor windows. With a cloth draping her cage, Nora slept peacefully. I heard a soft shuffling; a floorboard creaked in the upstairs hall.

I got up and went cautiously out of the dining room. The flight of stairs led directly into the parlor. It was bright enough for me to see a white shape on the landing. It halted for a few seconds, then floated down the steps.

It was Captain Jack in his underwear.

My grandmother had warned me never to wake him up when he was having one of his spells, so I stood there holding my breath. I hoped he would turn around and go back upstairs.

Captain Jack moved steadily through the parlor, heading straight for Nora's cage. Frozen to the spot, I could do nothing to stop him. He took another pace and lurched against the stand. It toppled over; the cage crashed to the floor.

11

Toys in the Cellar

ora beat her wings against the bars of the overturned
cage. Her water cup spilled, her sunflower seeds scat-
tered over the rug. She screamed at the top of her voice. Captain Jack began screaming, too. Upstairs, someone switched on
the parlor lights. My grandmother and The Gawgon, in their
summer nightgowns, came down the steps. I could only think
of setting the cage upright and covering it with the cloth. It did
not quiet her.

Captain Jack crouched on the floor amid the sunflower
seeds, knees tucked under his chin, hands pressed against his
ears. He was howling like a wolf. My grandmother, in tears, circled around him, begging him to be calm. She seemed afraid to
go any closer.

The Gawgon moved quickly. White hair unbraided and

hanging every which way, she went straight to him, knelt, and held him in her arms.

"Call McKelvie," she said sharply to my grandmother, and to me, "Go stay in the kitchen."

I obeyed, partially. I stopped in the middle of the dining room. Despite myself, I could not turn my eyes away. The Gawgon was stroking Captain Jack's head and rocking him back and forth.

It was dawn by the time Dr. McKelvie came, tousled, coat unbuttoned, without a cravat. Still in The Gawgon's arms, Captain Jack had stopped screaming and was merely sobbing. Dr. McKelvie opened his bag; I glimpsed a hypodermic needle in his hand.

"That's all I can do," he said to my grandmother. "I'll call the ambulance."

I ventured to the edge of the parlor. My grandmother went upstairs to fetch a bathrobe for Captain Jack. He was quiet now, but in spite of the injection, his eyes were wide open, the whites showing all around. When he happened to turn his head in my direction, he stared as if he had never seen me in all his life. I kept hoping he would at least recognize me; it had not been long ago when we listened to opera arias, when he called me "First Sergeant" and poured pancake syrup from a tin log cabin.

The men from the ambulance apologized, they were sorry to buckle him into a canvas straitjacket, but it was for his own good. Captain Jack did not struggle when they led him out of the house. He was well behaved and looked tired. In the street, he glanced around, squinting in the sunlight. The ambulance took him away.

Later, my grandmother went through the motions of fixing breakfast. None of us wanted any. We sat at the table for a while. I understood that Nora's squawking had set him off, but as I said apart to The Gawgon, I didn't see why Captain Jack got so upset. Nora, after all, was only a bird.

"She made him think of the war," The Gawgon said.

But that, I said, was over long ago.

"Not for Jack," The Gawgon answered. "He never talked about it to us. But his sister knew. She told us when she brought him to live here. She had to work all day, you see, so your grandmother promised to look after him. Something had happened that he never got out of his head."

I asked what it was.

The Gawgon did not answer right away. Then she said, "He was fond of you, and I know you were fond of him. Try to understand this. He shot his friend—

"No, it wasn't murder," The Gawgon quickly added, seeing the look on my face. "They were ordered out on a night patrol. A stupid order, no point in it. No doubt some general was bored and wanted to stir things up. The trenches were so close, the Germans saw them in the moonlight and opened fire.

"Jack was badly wounded; his friend, worse. The rest of the

patrol were dead. His friend kept screaming for Jack to shoot him, he couldn't stand the pain. Jack wouldn't do it. As his sister told us, they lay there a long time, with Jack's friend crying and begging to be put out of his misery.

"Jack hoped his friend would die soon, but he didn't. At the end, Jack shot him in the head with his revolver.

"When it was daylight, the Germans waved a flag of truce and let the Americans carry back the bodies. They all stayed in their own trenches after that. Jack was taken to a field hospital, and they sent him home."

I never thought of Captain Jack having relatives, but next weekend, I was at my grandmother's house when a plain-looking woman in a summer frock came to collect his belongings. She was his sister; my grandmother talked with her out of my earshot. Then a man came with a horse and cart to haul out the gramophone and records. The empty room still smelled of Turkish tobacco. The canvas window shades had been rolled up. I did not go in.

There was nothing else beyond some bundles of clothes and a few cardboard boxes in the cellar. I helped carry them up.

"I don't think he'll need any of this," my grandmother said.

"They're his things, even so," Captain Jack's sister said. "They're all he has."

Taking away the bundles left a gap like a tunnel in the heaps of odds and ends stacked against the cellar wall. One of my privileges was to root through whatever came to hand. Some days later, when things calmed down, I set about probing the tunnel.

Our cellar on Lorimer Street was too tidy to be interesting. My mother even dusted the chute, like a sliding board, that the coal man used to pour down chunks of coal into the storage bin. My grandmother's cellar, in contrast, was so disarrayed I could always find some surprise or other.

Most often, it was something with a vital part missing: a sewing machine treadle without the sewing machine; a reel of old movie film but no projector to show it; a couple of headless golf clubs; a gadget for clamping metal caps on homemade root beer, but no caps or bottles. Clues that my elders must have gone around playing golf, watching movies, drinking root beer, and leading glamorous lives of their own before I existed.

That morning, when I thought the vein of this particular mine was exhausted, from the deepest level I pulled out a wooden box. It rattled intriguingly. I, of course, lifted the lid. Inside lay a dozen or more toy soldiers, cast in lead, their paint still bright.

I immediately claimed possession. Leaving everything else strewn about the floor, I seized the box and galloped upstairs to show The Gawgon what I had unearthed.

The Gawgon was sitting at the rolltop desk. When I held out the box, she stiffened.

"Where did you get that, Boy?" she said in an odd voice.

As I began explaining, she took the little figures and stood them one by one on the desk.

"Union soldiers," she said. "There used to be Confederates, too, and horses.

"They all had their own names. I forget what they were." She picked up a blue-jacketed rifleman and turned it back and forth. "You found them, you can keep them."

I asked if they had been her toys.

The Gawgon gave a quick shake of her head. "My son's."

12

The Gawgon's Other Boy

"You didn't know? I'm surprised," she said, though I doubted she was half as surprised as I was.

"I assumed you already heard about it," The Gawgon said. "Family gossip—or so it used to be. Gossip, I suppose, goes out of date like everything else."

I expected her to change the subject, as my elders did when they caught me eavesdropping. Instead, she went on:

"His name was David, the same as yours. A quick, bright boy. You never knew what he'd be up to. He had a wild streak, like his father.

"He was close to your age when he died," The Gawgon said. "Influenza. They couldn't save him. That was the last time I saw his father. I wrote to him when it happened—he was always off to someplace or other. A wonder he came back at all."

The Gawgon's chin went up, her eyes flashed for an instant. Then her face softened. "No, I shouldn't say that. He did what he could. I was angry at him—for a little while. I could never stay angry at him very long. He was a charmer. And I? What did he call me? Intrepid? Fearless? Foolhardy, more like it.

"Yes," The Gawgon said, "he was the cheeky fellow who took my photo at the Pyramids. He kept trailing after me like a long-legged, overgrown puppy. I couldn't get rid of him. And didn't want to.

"We parted company in Cairo. When the tour ended, my employers didn't keep me on as a governess. I went home to Philadelphia.

"A few months later, that rascal came and found me. I was teaching school then. I had just come out of class and there he was, sitting on a bench in the hall. He asked if I remembered him. Oh, yes"—The Gawgon smiled—"I remembered him very well indeed.

"He wanted to be a photographer. That was the great new career in those days. He was going to Paris on the wild chance of studying with a Frenchman named Nadar, very famous at the time.

"He asked me to go with him," said The Gawgon. "Can you imagine? The nerve of the fellow! Standing there shuffling his feet, pretending to be shy—which he never was—with that loopy grin of his. I should give up my work and run off with a total stranger?

"I did, of course," said The Gawgon. "Yes, he was a

charmer. A footloose charmer. He thought staying in one place was a crime against nature; and I went along with him.

"He never did study with Nadar. He set up his own portrait studio in Paris. No sooner did we start doing well than we dashed away to look at castles in Spain or ride gondolas in Venice. Between times, I gave English lessons. He wrote travel articles for the newspapers—when he felt like it."

The Gawgon broke off and went to sit in the rocking chair. I waited, saying nothing. After a time, she looked up at me:

"When I knew I was expecting our child, I went home. He promised to join me later. He never got around to it. Mary—your grandmother—took me in. I've lived with her ever since.

"That was the last I saw of him until Davy died. He came back for three days. He wanted to stay longer, but he had started working as a foreign correspondent, always caught up in one thing or another. Good at his job, I'll say that much for him.

"He had gone gray by then, but as big a charmer as ever. He was too old for it, but when the war started he grinned his way into being a frontline photographer. Sometimes I'd have a letter from him. He was killed in France, in the Argonne Forest."

This was more than any adult had ever seen fit to tell me. I felt somehow blessed and grateful. And heartbroken for her. I expected to see her grief-stricken by her memories.

"What young fools we were," The Gawgon said. "If I had it

all to do over?" She paused and shook her head. "I'd do exactly the same. No, Boy, I don't regret one minute of it."

Her face was shining like a girl's.

I knew The Gawgon's opinion of Dr. McKelvie as a pill-roller and cheerful undertaker. He was, to me, a saint. The question came up again, at the end of summer, about my going back to Rittenhouse Academy. Dr. McKelvie strongly warned against it. So I was spared again, and I blessed him.

"Thank God for Annie," I heard my father say to my mother one evening. "That's a saving. Elise is taken care of, for now. At least, her term's paid in advance."

Much later, I understood why he seemed relieved. The store had not been doing well. Customers were not flocking to fill their houses with Oriental goods. On the contrary, they were staying away in large numbers.

"It's beyond me," my father said. "What are they doing? Buying cars? Playing the stock market?"

He did try something he was sure would excite public interest: Mexican jumping beans.

From one of his suppliers he bought a bushel of what looked like old peanuts with the reddish-brown skin still on them. They did not actually jump into the air, but they did twitch from time to time; some quite lively, others just sat there unwilling to do much of anything. He put a big platter of them in the store window and a bowlful on the counter next to the cash register.

"What it is," my father said—he had brought some home for our amusement—"there's a little worm inside. When it moves, the bean jumps."

"What do they do all day?" my mother asked. "Suppose they eat their way through the shell? They're going to come out and crawl all over the house."

"Don't worry," said my father. "It's never been known to happen."

Nevertheless, my mother did not like the idea of the worms being sealed up in a bean dungeon without air and sunlight. Tenderhearted by nature, she felt sorry for them. She wondered if she should slice open the beans and liberate the prisoners. They could live outside in the areaway.

"They're happy where they are," my father said. "Let them be. They're better off in Philadelphia than in Mexico."

The Mexican jumping beans had no connection with Oriental goods. But, my father pointed out, he was now the only source of jumping beans in Philadelphia; in effect, the jumping bean king.

He reckoned the beans would lure passersby into the store, giving him the chance to sell them other, and more expensive, merchandise.

After a couple of weeks, he realized his scheme was not working. The Mexican jumping beans made no difference at all; but having paid for them, he was not going to throw them out. He carried them home in a sack. He planned on keeping them for a return engagement in the spring, when he was sure they would do better.

To accommodate the beans, my mother put them in bowls and saucers throughout the house. They kept quietly to themselves, twitching occasionally.

The only excitement they produced was on an evening when Uncle Eustace stopped by to commiserate with my father. Uncle Eustace was having difficulties with tombstone sales. People were not dying as often as they should.

Uncle Eustace sat gloomily on the sofa. He kept dipping absentmindedly into a dish of beans on the end table. In his morose frame of mind, he no doubt mistook them for salted peanuts.

"Stop! Stop!" My mother gasped when she saw what he was doing. "They're full of worms!"

Uncle Eustace sprang to his feet and spat his mouthful of beans onto the Oriental rug.

"That's not funny, Dog Flea," he shouted at my father, who had burst out laughing.

Despite explanations from my mother, Uncle Eustace was still convinced my father meant to play a joke on him and went away in a huff.

The beans seemed comfortable in their new environment. My task, each morning, was to sprinkle them with water to keep them moist. I did this chore promptly and hurried to my lesson.

At my own request, we would now have longer sessions every weekday. My mother, astonished and delighted that I actually wanted to study, was also concerned that it would be too heavy a burden for an elderly person. But The Gawgon wholeheartedly agreed with the new plan.

" 'Summer's lease hath all too short a date'—that's Shakespeare," The Gawgon said. "We have a lot to do. We haven't even touched geometry—"

The first thing I knew about geometry was that my sister and the rest of the Tulip Garden flunked it. Second, it had to do with circles, triangles, and arithmetic. The simplest arithmetic was, to me, an inscrutable mystery. Throwing in circles and triangles made it horrifying. Since we had not yet touched geometry, I suggested not touching it at all.

"Oh, we'll touch it," said The Gawgon. "Whether you'll grasp it remains to be seen. When you come right down to it, geometry's really learning how to think. If you can learn how to think, you can learn how to learn. If you can learn how to learn, you can learn anything."

So, through autumn, The Gawgon began working me harder than ever, not forgetting to chivy me about the still-untangled yarn. During these longer sessions, her face would gather a few more wrinkles, she would stop and shut her eyes; then, taking a long breath, pick up where she left off. When I was especially dim-witted or The Gawgon especially tired, we put everything aside.

" 'Much study is a weariness of the flesh,' " The Gawgon said. "That's from the Bible—Ecclesiastes, if I'm not mistaken."

No longer confining herself to her room, The Gawgon decreed an occasional recess. Early autumn was warm and sungilded. Those days we strolled a couple of blocks to Elm Park, as it was called, though not an elm was to be found.

"There used to be elms, but they died off and had to be cut down," The Gawgon said as we sat on a bench. "There were still a few when Davy—my Davy—and I came here."

She opened a brown paper bag of bread crusts that my grandmother had given us and we tossed them to the resident pigeons. The Gawgon, since first telling me, had said nothing more about her son. But I had thought about him. On the one hand, I wished I had met him; on the other—yes, I admitted to myself I was a little jealous.

"You'd have liked him," The Gawgon went on as the pigeons flocked around. "Two of a kind—no, I take that back. He was one of a kind. Just as you're one of a kind."

I felt reassured by that. I had wondered if The Gawgon volunteered to teach me because I reminded her of the other Davy. I hesitated, then ventured to ask.

"Bless you, no," The Gawgon said. "What's gone is gone. Sometimes we lose what we love best. The way of the world, Boy. We always keep loving and remembering, but the past isn't a good place to live in, only to visit from time to time.

"No," she said, "I wanted to teach you because I suspected

you had the makings of a good mind. What you may do with it, I can't guess. But you deserve a chance to make something of yourself. I'll see that you get one."

The pigeons had been flapping all around us. One brazenly perched on The Gawgon's shoulder, and she let it peck crumbs from her hand.

When the bag was empty, our recess ended. We started back with the pigeons trailing hopefully behind. A street cleaner in a white uniform was sweeping up the leaves with a long-handled brush and piling them into pyramids of red and orange.

"I see nothing sad about falling leaves," The Gawgon remarked. "New ones always come along. What did that poet— Oliver Wendell Holmes—say about the last leaf on the tree?

Let them smile, as I do now,
At the old forsaken bough
Where I cling.

"And I," said The Gawgon, "intend to cling for a good long time. It may take a good long time to squeeze any sense into you."

It always made me uneasy when my relatives spoke politely to each other. It usually meant something serious was in the wind. One rainy night at the end of October, Uncle Rob, without Aunt Rosie, came to Lorimer Street. My father helped him off with his coat.

"Thank you, Rob, for coming out in this weather." My father ushered him into the dining room, where my mother already sat at the table. "We can't rightly talk about this on the phone.

"It could have some effect on your mother's situation," my father went on. "Some effect on all of us, for that matter. You should know what I'm thinking. I'd be glad for your opinion."

They murmured back and forth under the glow of the chandelier. My mother jotted figures on sheets of paper.

Something had gone wrong with the stock market. I did not know what the stock market was, except my father found it intensely interesting. It had collapsed, crashed, or some such.

I could get no mental picture of a market crashing, apart from shelves in the grocery store falling down and canned vegetables rolling around, so I could not follow the conversation.

"Sound reasoning, Alan," Uncle Rob said at last. "I agree. But, as you well know, it's unwise to move too quickly. The market will bounce back. President Hoover will make sure it does."

Uncle Rob and my mother embraced, my father shook hands, thanked him again, and he went home.

Uncle Rob, for the first time, did not slip me a quarter.

13

The Consulting Detective

Mrs. Jossbegger died in November. My grandmother and The Gawgon did not feel up to a funeral. Leaving me with them, my mother and my aunts attended the service. They had put on the black dresses they kept available for sad occasions. Afterward, my mother reported it was nicely done. Aunt Rosie thought it was skimpy.

"I'm sure they did the best they could," my mother said. "Everyone's cutting back, these days."

"Cutting back? On funerals?" Aunt Rosie said. "Heaven help us, where will it all end?"

Mrs. Jossbegger's absence ended the corn-cutting sessions. As for the stock market crash, Uncle Rob's visit troubled me. I privately asked my sister about it.

"If you paid attention to something besides drawing those

dumb pictures, you wouldn't have to ask," she said—which meant she understood no more than I did.

What, I wondered, had it to do with our grandmother?

"You really are the stupidest blighter," my sister said. "Don't you know anything at all? Grandmother counts on Father to help out. She has to. She doesn't make enough money from the lodgers. The house doesn't even belong to her."

I had never heard about that. "Whose is it?"

"Father's," my sister said. "That's right. He owns it. He lets her live there free, but it's still his house. He buys stocks for her, too. That must be what he and Uncle Rob were talking about.

"Father will take care of everything," she went on. "Anyhow, it's got nothing to do with blighters. It's none of your business."

My sister knew the hallways and back stairs of the adult world, so I believed her. But if it was none of my business, all the more reason to make it so.

Next time I saw The Gawgon, I asked her to explain the puzzling crash. She tried her best; still I did not grasp it, only that it was not good.

"No, it isn't good," The Gawgon said. "Something like it happened before, years ago, and that was very bad, too. It all worked out in the end. I hope it works out again. President Hoover says it will. But when politicians promise everything's going to be rosy, I start feeling my pockets."

I let it go at that. I would make it my business some other time. I had enough crowding my head. As threatened, The

Gawgon dipped me into geometry. If this was supposed to teach me to think, it felt more like frying my brain. The notion of pi, a number that could stretch out endlessly, bewildered me. But at least I was good at drawing circles.

The Gawgon could sense when my mind wandered hopelessly beyond her reach. To give me some relief from theorems and propositions, she handed me a book of mystery stories.

"Better than just mysteries," she said. "Sherlock Holmes can show you how to pay attention to details and figure things out logically.

"Arthur Conan Doyle started out as a doctor," The Gawgon said. "He wrote to pass the time between patients. Since he didn't have a lot of patients, he ended up writing a lot of stories. His old professor was his inspiration for Sherlock Holmes, the world's greatest consulting detective."

It wasn't long before I was so captivated by Sherlock Holmes, I half believed he and his companion, Dr. Watson, really existed.

"They do," she said. "In your imagination."

Though devoted to him, I decided Holmes was not the world's greatest consulting detective. Second greatest. First was: The Gawgon.

THE AFFAIR OF THE SEATED KING

*T*he dense fog, which makes London infamous throughout the world, was so heavy as to be impenetrable. The entire city lay immobilized. Horses balked at pulling their hansom cabs. Police constables, attempting to walk their beats, became hopelessly lost and confused. The crowded streets were now deserted. Thieves and pickpockets, who normally thronged Belgrave Square and Piccadilly Circus, remained within their sordid lairs.

Unusual even by London standards, the fog discouraged us from taking our afternoon stroll in Kensington Gardens, and so The Gawgon and I chose to stay in our apartments, with a cheery coal fire in the grate, and amused ourselves by solving problems in geometry.

The Gawgon found the square of the hypotenuse to be especially droll and entertaining. We were chuckling over it when Miss Florry, our smartly attired housekeeper, announced the arrival of a gentleman identifying himself as Mr. Hemlock Soames.

Without waiting for permission, this individual brushed past Miss Florry and entered our sitting room.

"I pray you will forgive this unconscionable intrusion." The unexpected visitor removed his black bowler hat and made a courteous bow. He was tall and lean, almost gaunt. A pair of pince-nez spectacles bridged the high arch of his nose. His pale brow seemed to radiate a cool inner light.

"It is all the more unpardonable"—his quick eyes scanned the papers on the writing table—"since I observe you and your colleague are deeply engrossed in the square of the hypotenuse, which I myself always find a most enjoyable diversion.

"Be sure," he added, "only a matter of extreme urgency brings me to impose my presence so rudely upon you."

The Gawgon, in a watered-silk dressing gown, approached him and shook his hand, and with her usual graciousness, invited him to sit in our best upholstered armchair.

"Before you reveal your difficulty," said The Gawgon, "it is essential to deal with each other in total frankness.

"You, I have reason to believe," she went on, offering him a goblet of soda water, "are endeavoring to practice a small deception upon us."

The gentleman startled and choked on his soda water as The Gawgon continued:

"I detect a slight West Indian accent in your speech. Jamaica rather than Trinidad; Kingston rather than Montego Bay. But, as well, I hear a charming musicality unique to that great American metropolis Philadelphia. Curious combination. It is possible, of course, that you have traveled or resided in those areas. A diplomat? A statesman? No, I discern too much intelligence in your features. You have, perhaps, assumed these accents for misleading purposes.

"Also, you appreciate the subtle joys of the square of the hypotenuse; therefore, I doubt that you are an ordinary plainclothes policeman in the employ of Scotland Yard.

"More conclusively," went on The Gawgon, "I notice an odor—I refrain from calling it a stench—of pipe tobacco about your person. A private blend of Latakia and Egyptian? Further, when shaking your hand, I felt a small callus near the second knuckle of your index finger, caused, I hypothesize, by long use of the bow for a stringed instrument. Were I to examine your left hand, I am convinced I should find other calluses on your fingertips. You play the cello, violin, or viola—most likely, the violin.

"Finally, with the exception of myself, only one person knows every inch of London so well that he could make his way blindfolded—or, in this case, fogbound.

"For the sake of accuracy, I prefer to address you by your true name: Mr. Sherlock Holmes."

"Touché!" exclaimed Sherlock Holmes. "My compliments. I consider myself—I do not indulge in false modesty—a master of disguise. I should have known The Gawgon would see through my masquerade."

"Now that your identity has been established," said The Gawgon, "allow me to inquire: Why did you come disguised in the first place?"

"I was obliged to do so," replied Holmes. "There are always watching eyes and listening ears. If it became known that you were associated with me in any way, or that we have so much as spoken together, your life would be at risk as well as mine. For your own protection, I dared not take the chance of being recognized. I must warn you in advance: This affair is dangerous in the extreme."

"Risk, my dear sir, is what makes life interesting," said The Gawgon. "Now, I trust, you will explain the nature of this perilous situation."

"To put it briefly," replied Holmes, "after long and difficult negotiations, the Greek government has finally consented to lend the British Museum, for exhibition, its rarest and greatest treasure.

"It is a lifesize statue, the ultimate masterpiece by that sublime sculptor, Phidias. You are familiar, of course, with the mythical hero Perseus, who brought the head of Medusa to King Polydectes. At sight of it, the king was instantly turned to stone.

"The statue represents the king, seated on his throne, reaching out a hand to receive Medusa's head. The throne, alas, has not survived the ravages of time, but the figure is intact.

"It is superb," Holmes went on. "A glory of classical antiquity, a consummate work of art. Its value—beyond price. The ministry in Athens, reluctant to lend it in the first place, is profoundly concerned for its safety."

"Understandably," said The Gawgon. "If any harm were to befall this treasure, I foresee that Greece would be outraged, even to a point of threatening war. The Balkans, naturally, would be drawn in; the Russians would take a hand; the French could not resist meddling, which would stir up the Austrians and Prussians. In effect, a catastrophe. The object must be protected at all cost."

"You analyze it perfectly," said Holmes. "One thing I have not mentioned: The statue has already been stolen."

14

My Uncle Santa Claus

The following Thursday, everyone ate Thanksgiving dinner at my grandmother's: a very good dinner, as it always was. My mother declared we had a great deal to be thankful for: We were better off than a lot of people; we were indoors eating instead of outdoors starving; and things could be worse. This, of course, was absolutely true and we were grateful. Still, nobody was having much of a laughing time.

My father and Uncle Rob sat deep in conversation. My sister, bored, would rather have been with her Tulip Garden. Aunt Marta dozed in a chair, never attempting even a chorus of "Sari Marais." The Gawgon, suffering a touch of indigestion, went to her room. Uncle Will, who had another engagement, left right after the mince pie. The only one in good spirits was Uncle Eustace. The raw weather had perked up the tombstone business; he was close to being lighthearted, and he had forgiven my father for feeding him the Mexican jumping beans.

In the kitchen, my mother, grandmother, Aunt Rosie, and Aunt Florry did the dishes. My work was to dry the silverware, a task that for some reason I disliked, and I was impatient to be done. Aunt Florry, usually brisk in washing up, was slow about it and, at one point, stopped altogether.

"I'll tell the men later." Aunt Florry kept wiping her hands on her apron. "Will can explain more when he comes back."

"Mrs. Heberton had to let us go."

"What? Fired?" Aunt Rosie burst out before my grandmother could say anything. "Both of you? After all these years, just like that? Ha! There's your high muckety-mucks, riding roughshot over everybody!"

"Oh, Florry, this is too bad." My grandmother put her arms around her. "Why? What happened? I never thought for a moment—"

"She couldn't help it," Aunt Florry said. "She certainly didn't want to. She's been talking with Mr. Ormond at her bank; he takes care of all her business. He's doing his best for her, but she'll have to close the house and try to sell it when the market's better. She can't afford to keep it up, least of all paying a companion and a chauffeur."

"With her money?" retorted Aunt Rosie.

"Not anymore," said Aunt Florry. "She'll be lucky if she comes out with a penny to her name. Until things turn better, she's going to live with her son in New Jersey."

"Serves her right," Aunt Rosie declared. "That's mean, firing people at the holidays."

"No, she was very generous," Aunt Florry said. "Mrs. Heberton paid us to the middle of January. She didn't have to do that. She knows a lot of people, she promised she'd ask around and see if she could find jobs for us.

"I feel so bad for Will," Aunt Florry went on. "He was happy there, driving the car and looking after the grounds. He never touched a drop when he was working."

"If you need a place to stay—" my mother began.

"You'll stay here," my grandmother told Aunt Florry. "In Jack's room. I still don't have the heart to rent it to strangers. I'll fix up something for Will, too."

Everybody went home soon after. We walked the few blocks to Lorimer Street; my mother thought the exercise would be good for our digestion. My father and mother talked between themselves. My sister, sulking, trudged behind.

It began to drizzle; the streetlights were pale smears. Most of the neighborhood street lamps, in those days, were gas. Just before sundown, a man came with a lighter on the end of a pole; mornings, he came back and snuffed out the flame. Now, with the mist swirling around the alleyways, it was the ideal place for lurking assassins; and Sherlock Holmes's mortal enemy, Professor Moriarty, was probably stalking us. I turned into the shadows of Lorimer Street as if I had never been there before.

AN EXPENSIVE TAILOR

Yes," Holmes said flatly, "the priceless statue of King Polydectes has been stolen. It was stored in the basement of the British Museum for minor cleaning and restoration. Now it has vanished. The theft, so far, has not been made public, but you understand the consequences if its disappearance is revealed."

"And you, sir," I put in, "must find out who stole it."

"Of course not," said Holmes, with some asperity at my naive remark. "I know that fact already.

"I have, an hour ago, received a message from the perpetrator," Holmes went on. "A taunting communication, indeed. He boasts that he has planned it all in advance. He chooses to toy with me and play a vicious game. He challenges me to recover the statue within twenty-four hours.

"Otherwise, he will send an open letter to the *Times* and all foreign embassies, thus lighting the fuse of the European powder keg. Worse, when the disaster is revealed, London's thousands of painters, poets, novelists, and other devoted art lovers will riot in the streets. A terrifying prospect.

"Scotland Yard is incompetent to deal with the case," Holmes continued. "The blame will be laid on my failure."

"Diabolical!" I exclaimed. "What fiendish intelligence conceived such a plot?"

"One man," replied Holmes. "That individual who tirelessly seeks my destruction, who has already tried to murder me: Professor Moriarty."

The Gawgon nodded. "The Napoleon of crime."

"None other," said Holmes. "When you observed that only you and I could make our way through London's worst fog, you should have included Moriarty and his hirelings. Nothing keeps them from their loathsome business."

"Very possibly he means to draw you out and strike at your person," The Gawgon said, "but it would merely add a little icing to his poisonous confection: desirable but not essential. Destroying your reputation is far crueler than destroying you corporeally."

"I am aware of that," said Sherlock Holmes. "Alas, my staunch companion, Dr. Watson, has been called away for a fortnight in Wolverhampton. My brother Mycroft, though a genius, is preoccupied with philosophical speculations. Nothing, not even the fate of the world, could induce him to venture from the reading room of his club. And so I turn to you for any suggestion or advice you may wish to offer."

"My suggestion is this," The Gawgon said, after a few moments of reflection. "Return immediately to your Baker Street apartments. Do not, in any circumstances, leave them until you receive word from us. My advice: Put this matter entirely in the hands of The Boy and myself."

Although Holmes protested, unwilling for us to risk our lives, he at last, and most reluctantly, agreed. Once the great detective had left our premises, The Gawgon went to her filing cabinet, where she riffled through the folders.

"Ah, yes, here it is: the key to a secret entrance of the

British Museum." She winked at me. "I doubt that even Mr. Sherlock Holmes has such a means of access."

From her wardrobe of disguises, she outfitted us with black bowler hats, dark suits, tightly furled umbrellas, and Old School ties.

"From among the thousands of merchant bankers and stockbrokers wearing this identical garb," she said, "it will be impossible for Moriarty to pick us out."

I mentioned she had neglected to take revolvers from her extensive arsenal.

"If my hypothesis is correct, firearms will not be necessary," she said. "Come along, Boy. The game's afoot."

In the streets, we made our way unerringly through the enveloping fog. Arriving at the rear of the British Museum, The Gawgon produced her key and opened a narrow door. We went swiftly down the empty corridors lit by the occasional gas jet. As familiar with the bowels of the British Museum as she was with our own apartments, The Gawgon entered a room where various implements covered a worktable.

"Yes, the statue was brought here and set on this bench." The Gawgon lit a gas lamp, took a magnifying glass from her pocket, and scrutinized the area.

"I see traces of parallel lines on the floor," she said. "As Euclid points out, parallel lines do not meet, and so I assume these tracks continue—"

I had, in the meantime, noticed a crumpled scrap of paper

under the worktable. I hurried to pick it up and hand it to The Gawgon. She smoothed it out and studied it closely.

"Well done, Boy. This is a better stroke of luck than I could have hoped. Even a master criminal has moments of carelessness. It makes my work much easier, for the pieces of the puzzle now begin falling into place. This may confirm what I privately theorized from the start.

"It is a bill, quite a large bill," said The Gawgon, "from Houndstooth & Son, the most elegant and expensive tailors on Savile Row. I believe, Boy, it tells us all we need to know."

———————

"Will wants to be Santa Claus," my grandmother said, later that day.

My mother and Aunt Florry were back from shopping on Fifty-second Street. I had just come down from The Gawgon's room and was as surprised as they were. Uncle Will had not been Santa Claus for several years now.

"If he'd like to," my mother said, "of course, let him do it."

"Do we still have the suit and the beard?" asked Aunt Florry.

"Packed away. I'll air them out," my grandmother said. "It was Will's idea," she added. "He wants this to be a good Christmas."

When I still fervently believed in him and loved him, Santa Claus always came to visit. We would gather in my grandmother's parlor to wait for him on Christmas Eve. Uncle Will would always be there, eager as the rest of us, but he kept looking at his wristwatch.

"He's late," Uncle Will would say at last. "I have to run an errand. I'll be right back."

"Better hurry," my grandmother warned. "You don't want to miss him."

Uncle Will put on his hat and coat and left the house. I was fidgety, afraid he might not come back in time. But—and it happened fatefully every year—after about twenty minutes, there were loud knockings at the door.

"Santa Claus? My goodness!" My grandmother clapped her hands to her head. "And Will's not here!"

She opened the door. Santa Claus came rolling in, red-suited, with bouncing belly, a white beard up to his eyes, a sack over his shoulder. He boomed out some ho-ho-hos, then suddenly stopped.

"Someone's missing." Santa Claus glanced around. "I don't see Will."

My grandmother explained that Will had gone on a short errand. Santa said he would catch up with him later. He heaved himself into an armchair; my sister and I sat on his knees while he fished out small presents from his sack, which looked suspiciously like a pillowcase.

We begged him to wait, Uncle Will would be here at any moment. But Santa had other stops to make; he bustled out with a flurry of ho-hos and Merry Christmases. Soon after, Uncle

Will came back. When he found out he had missed Santa Claus, he sighed with huge regret.

"Next year," he said. "Next year for sure."

It did not happen. He missed the visit every Christmas. But except for Uncle Will's annual disappointment, these were always magical evenings. In addition to the smells of mince and pumpkin pies, the sage and onions of turkey stuffing, another aroma floated in the air, the very essence of Santa Claus.

Years later, when I was grown up, I still remembered that marvelous fragrance and recognized it as Scotch whisky.

15

Simple Gifts

hen I was about seven or eight, Uncle Will stopped disappearing on Christmas Eve and Santa Claus stopped visiting. By then, I learned that Uncle Will's annual errand was a quick trip next door to the Noonans. Santa's costume and sack of presents were already there; he simply dressed up in the red suit and beard and hurried back.

I missed his visits. Now that Uncle Will decided on a return performance, even knowing what I knew, I was eager to see Santa Claus again. Though he was not the genuine article, it made no difference. As The Gawgon had said about Sherlock Holmes, Santa lived where he should: in my imagination.

As for Holmes, amid all the Christmas preparations I had

neglected him; he was still cooling his heels at Baker Street, where The Gawgon had sent him.

THE PANJANDRUM CLUB

*B*y the time The Gawgon and I left the British Museum, the fog had lifted and the skies had cleared to their usual sooty gray, the nearest thing to a sparkle that London could produce. Carefully pocketing the tailor's bill from Houndstooth & Son, The Gawgon directed me to return to our chambers. "On the way, would you be so kind as to take a message to Mr. Sherlock Holmes?" she said. "If he is interested in learning the whereabouts of the stolen statue of King Polydectes, he is invited to join us at high noon.

"He need not disguise himself," she added. "Also, assure him tea will be served."

The Gawgon declined my offer to accompany her. "Time presses. Professor Moriarty is surely gloating, impatient to set his diabolical scheme in motion. Some tasks remain, I can accomplish them more promptly alone."

She vanished into the throng of bowler-hatted, umbrella-bearing stockbrokers. Much as I wished to observe her brilliant analytical mind at work, I followed her instructions, then waited for the appointed hour.

Sherlock Holmes arrived a few moments early, for which he apologized. He wore his famous cape and the cloth cap of the style known as a deerstalker. No sooner had he entered than Big Ben boomed out noon. Before the echoes of the twelfth stroke died away, The Gawgon appeared.

Holmes sprang to his feet. "Dear lady, I am relieved to see you unharmed. Your message led me to hope—"

"Do you take milk or lemon in your tea?" The Gawgon deposited her umbrella in the Ming vase at the door. "Ah, yes. The location of the statue? Set your mind at ease, Mr. Holmes. King Polydectes is exactly where he belongs."

"Good heavens!" exclaimed Holmes. "That would be—?"

"On proud display in the British Museum. Even as we speak, crowds are gathering to admire this treasure. Europe has been spared a conflict and Professor Moriarty foiled again."

"A brilliant accomplishment! As to be expected from The Gawgon and The Boy," said Holmes. "My gratitude is beyond expression. Let me ask one thing more: Your method of solving this most difficult and puzzling case?"

"Elementary." The Gawgon handed him the tailor's bill that I had found. "Thanks to The Boy, this was my first significant clue. All else followed logically.

"It immediately occurred to me," The Gawgon continued, "that the humble employees of the British Museum are in no financial position to patronize expensive tailors."

"Certainly not," agreed Holmes.

"Therefore, my suspicions were aroused," said The Gawgon. "I went immediately to Houndstooth & Son. They recalled making the suit, but what engraved it indelibly on their mind was something altogether bizarre.

"The customer did not come personally to be fitted. Instead, an arrogant, sneering sort of individual—by now, I was sure it was Moriarty—brought a list of measurements: waist, height, inside leg, and so on. Mr. Houndstooth showed me the specifications. They corresponded exactly to the dimensions of King Polydectes.

"At that moment, I grasped the nature of Moriarty's scheme, fiendish in its simplicity, simple in its fiendishness." The Gawgon turned to me. "Do you remember the parallel tracks on the floor? Close examination showed me they had been made by a wheelchair, probably what is called a 'Bath chair,' fitted with a small hood or canopy.

"For the rest"—The Gawgon shrugged—"a matter of logical deduction. Moriarty had several of his henchmen wheel him into the museum; a common enough sight, an invalid being taken on a cultural outing, nothing to arouse suspicion. They concealed themselves until the museum closed, then entered the basement, dressed the statue in its custom-tailored suit, and set it in the chair. Next morning, mingling with the crowd, they wheeled King Polydectes out of the building. The theft was accomplished."

"So it must have been!" cried Holmes. "A magnificent reconstruction of the crime. But, my dear Gawgon, the crucial question is: What did Moriarty do with the statue?"

"Easily answered," said The Gawgon. "You are, of course, familiar with the principle: The best hiding place is in plain sight."

"Correct," said Holmes. "When an object blends so naturally with its surroundings, it becomes, in a practical sense, invisible. But a marble statue wearing a Savile Row suit?"

"You know the Panjandrum Club, the oldest gentleman's club in London," The Gawgon said as Holmes nodded. "Its members are as ancient and decrepit as the institution itself; their average age, according to my research, is ninety-seven.

"Moriarty and his henchmen simply wheeled the statue only a block away to the Panjandrum Club and into the reading room. I interviewed the doorman and the steward, both doddering and dim-eyed, who swore they recognized King Polydectes as a member. The equally aged waiter, glimpsing the king's outstretched hand, automatically put a glass of brandy in it, brought a copy of the *Times,* and spread it on his lap. There was, then, no observable difference between the statue and the rest of the Panjandrum's members, most of them already petrified in Bath chairs.

"I confirmed this for myself," said The Gawgon. "Once I explained what was at stake, I was allowed to enter the reading room. Since the club's ironbound rule is never to disturb a member, Polydectes still sat there, glass in hand, apparently reading a *Times* editorial, and from his stony glare, disagreeing with it.

"I then notified the museum staff. With utmost discretion,

they sent custodians to wheel out the statue and bring it to the exhibit hall, where it now resides in all its glory. The custom-tailored suit, naturally, was removed.

"And so, Mr. Holmes, the case is closed. It was our pleasure to be of some small assistance."

"For me, more than a pleasure," said Holmes, rising to his feet. "It has been the highest privilege." He bowed to me and bestowed a gallant kiss on The Gawgon's hand.

"You are, of course, uniquely The Gawgon," he said, with something warmer than admiration. "But, to me, you will always be: The Woman."

"I take that as a compliment," said The Gawgon.

"Elementary," I said.

Thuh End

Next day was Christmas Eve. At Uncle Will's request—and since he was to be Santa Claus again, it was happily granted—we rearranged the usual order of events. This year, we would not exchange gifts on Christmas Eve. Santa would arrive on Christmas Day, after dinner, and distribute everybody's presents from his pillowcase.

Uncle Will, meantime, had bought a handsome Christmas tree and trimmed most of it himself, with some added help from Aunt Florry and me. Nora got more and more excited at the shining ornaments, the ones we used every year; whooping and whistling, she tried to flap onto the top of the tree and had to be put in her cage. She made me think of Captain Jack, who once said she ought to be roasted for Christmas. I missed Captain Jack, but from what I understood, he was in some kind of hospital and would be there a long time.

Aunt Rosie was, at first, leery of the new plan.

"I don't like changing things around," she confided to my mother. "I hope it doesn't do something to my digestive track."

Nevertheless, she got herself into the spirit of the occasion and forgot about her digestive tract. Aunt Marta, carried away by the festivities, spontaneously burst into song, pleading to be taken back to the old Transvaal. Uncle Eustace, instead of grumbling, called for an encore. He was in fine fettle, selling more tombstones than he expected.

Uncle Rob, in addition to taking care of family legal matters, served as official turkey-carver and did it very well. It was, all in all, the liveliest and best Christmas feast I remembered.

Now the secret was known, I thought Uncle Will would simply go upstairs after dinner and put on the Santa Claus suit, but he claimed his usual errand and ducked out of the house. Soon after, Santa arrived. We cheered like wild and clapped our hands. He plumped into the armchair, I sat on one knee, my sister—grown long-legged since his last visit—perched awkwardly on the other. Again, the cloud of marvelous Santa Claus aroma enveloped me.

Uncle Will opened the pillowcase. This time, it held everybody's presents wrapped and tagged. He picked them out one by one and called our names. Before handing them around, he made a great to-do, shaking them, turning them upside down, pretending to guess what they were.

"This looks like a radio." Uncle Will held up a narrow box that could only contain a necktie. He hefted another package. "What's this? A new car?"

I had neither money nor access to department stores, so my mother bought gifts on my behalf. For a long time, I believed older ladies yearned for bags of sachet and jars of potpourri. That was what I always gave my grandmother and The Gawgon, and they were enraptured. I was also led to believe my aunts could wish for nothing finer than a slip, which I gave them. As it turned out, they all gave each other slips, were overjoyed, and held these undergarments in front of themselves for everyone to admire.

Two gifts came as no surprise. A couple of years before, my father had given Uncle Eustace a wooden bowl of shaving soap, and Uncle Eustace had given my father a straw-covered bottle of bay-rum face lotion. My father hated bay rum, even though it came from the West Indies. The following Christmas, he rewrapped the bottle and gave it back to Uncle Eustace.

"He won't remember," my father assured my mother.

That same Christmas, Uncle Eustace gave my father the wooden bowl of shaving soap.

Neither one said a word about it. From then on, they kept exchanging the bay rum and shaving soap, thanking each other and declaring it was just what they always wanted.

My sister and I already had our major presents at home on Lorimer Street. Here, I mostly received the dreaded underwear. But The Gawgon gave me a spectacular gift: one of her own books, a large-sized history of the world, filled with engravings of Egyptians, Greeks, and Romans. It was the first of three volumes. From the Sphinx-like smile on her face, I had reason to hope the others would someday be forthcoming.

I had my own extra, secret present for The Gawgon. I handed it to her when no one was looking and whispered she should unwrap it later.

When the pillowcase was empty, Uncle Will stood up and declared he had a lot of other visits to make. He embraced each of us. His white beard had gone crooked, but nobody minded.

He stopped at the door, blew kisses, and waved his arms.

"Ho-ho-ho!" he boomed. "Merry Christmas, God bless us every one!"

Next morning, Uncle Will packed a valise and left. It was the last we would see of him.

16

A Present for The Gawgon

I knew Will was leaving," my grandmother said. "He told me two weeks ago."

My mother and I had come for the usual after-Christmas lunch of leftovers. With Aunt Rosie, we sat around the kitchen table while Aunt Florry made up platters of cold turkey and stuffing. The Gawgon was still in her room.

"He didn't have the heart to tell anyone else," my grandmother added. "It hurt him too much. He simply couldn't do it. That's why he wanted to be Santa Claus again. It was his way of saying good-bye. He's right, there's nothing for him here. He's going west."

My mother and Aunt Florry looked choked up; Uncle Will was their favorite, as he was everyone's. Aunt Rosie flung down the turkey wing she had been nibbling:

"West? And be a cowboy buggaroo? What's he thinking?"

"Not the *West*. Pittsburgh," my grandmother said. "Or Detroit, if the auto plants are still hiring."

"He should go on to Hollywood," Aunt Rosie declared. "All those movie stars need chauffeurs."

"He doesn't want to be a chauffeur anymore," my grandmother said. "Will's a man of his hands. He'll find something."

The adults began talking over my head, so I went upstairs to visit The Gawgon.

She had not yet opened her secret present, waiting until I was there. Half hopeful, half shy, I watched as she carefully peeled off the wrapping to save for next Christmas.

I had gathered all the pictures I had sketched during the past months. I used red construction paper for the covers, punched holes on one side, and wove red yarn through them; the best I could think of for a handsome, special gift.

The Gawgon turned the pages. I began wishing I had never done it, for it suddenly looked shabby. But she smiled and, a few times, laughed out loud.

"So, that's what you've been up to when you should have been thinking about your lessons," she said, with a touch of severity. Then her eyes twinkled. "It's a lovely present. Thank you, Boy."

The Gawgon put her arms around me and kissed me on the cheek, which was the first time she had ever done that. Then she went back to studying the pictures, holding them out at arm's length.

"You might have a talent for this," she said. "More than you do for geometry."

I told her I could also make cootie-catchers.

The Gawgon ignored that and looked appraisingly at the drawings. "One thing," she said, "you have a good feeling for movement in the figures. Not easily learned, but you have a natural sense of it. And personality, which is something that can't be learned at all.

"For the rest, a lot of details are out of kilter. See here, you tried to draw a rocking chair—I suppose that's me sitting in it, but we'll let that pass—but the way you've done it, the chair can't rock. You need to look hard at things. Understand how they work before you start drawing them.

"It wouldn't hurt you to study great paintings and see what the old masters did. I have some postcards. They'll teach you more than I can."

The Gawgon put my collection on her desk. "You're a clever boy. You might end up being an artist—though I'm not sure I'd wish that on you. It can break your heart. It usually does."

Since no one was in the mood for it, we did not celebrate New Year's beyond listening to the radio and staying up until midnight. The Gawgon put off our lessons for a couple of days. Next time we met, her face was chalky, she was in a flannel bathrobe and out of sorts.

"McKelvie, that fool! What does he expect me to do?" The Gawgon muttered. "Live like a vegetable?"

She brought out the postcards she had talked about, and we picked through them. She held up a picture of a woman doing nothing in particular except sitting and vaguely smiling.

"Her name is Lisa del Giocondo. Mona Lisa, for short," The Gawgon said. "The most famous portrait in the world. An Italian painted her, something like four hundred years ago."

The Gawgon, growing more animated, went on about the artist, Leonardo da Vinci. Not only his pictures but, as well, his botanical and anatomical studies, plans for buildings, canals, even a flying machine. It amazed me to think he had designed an airplane hundreds of years ahead of anybody else. Still, I kept glancing at Mona Lisa, who smiled back as if she knew something important and wouldn't tell me.

"She does tease you," The Gawgon said. "She teases everybody. Leonardo, greatest genius of his day, had a thousand things on his mind. But she haunted him. He never got free of her."

TIC-TAC-TOE

We were in Venice, in The Gawgon's palazzo overlooking the Grand Canal, when a nice letter arrived from the Pope.

The Gawgon, beautifully regal in a gown decorated with seed pearls, scanned the page.

"He invites us to have dinner with him," she said. "Well, why not? He isn't a jolly table companion, but he has a first-rate cook.

"I'd thought of going to Rome anyway. They've discovered

a rare ancient mural; it should be interesting. Better yet, we'll stop off in Florence. That's the real city for artists. They have more painters than pigeons. We can see the Pope when we get around to it."

We set off, next day, in The Gawgon's splendidly outfitted coach and four, reaching Florence by leisurely stages. I had never seen the city before. However, instead of admiring its many picturesque tourist attractions, The Gawgon drove to a large, handsome house, with courtyard and gardens. The housekeeper was happy to see her, but when The Gawgon asked if Ser da Vinci was at home, her face fell.

"In the studio," she said. "He won't come out. He sits, he stares. *Malocchio!* I tell you someone put the evil eye on him."

"We'll see about that," said The Gawgon.

She left her traveling cloak and floppy velvet hat with the housekeeper, and we made our way to a big, airy room at the back of the house. I expected to find paintings and sketches covering the walls. They stood bare. The studio was empty of furnishings except for a chair and a nearby easel.

The artist himself sat hunched at a table covered with papers, scratching away with a stick of charcoal. He was fair-complexioned, with a curled mustache and neatly trimmed beard, a generous, noble brow, and a receding hairline.

"*Ciao,* Leo," said The Gawgon.

He started, ready to throw something. Recognizing The Gawgon, he jumped out of his chair and hurried to greet us.

"La Bella Gaugonna!" he exclaimed, embracing her. "*Ben-*

venuta! It's been too long already. This is The Boy, Il Ragazzo? Aie, *misericordia,* you find me not at my best."

"How so?" said The Gawgon. "What's wrong?"

"Don't ask," said Leonardo.

"Come, now," said The Gawgon. "I hear you've been doing pretty well for yourself. You're the most famous artist in Florence."

"City of jackals!" Leonardo made a gesture with his fingers that only an Italian can fill with such intense emotion. "And the worst of them—that ham-fisted stonecutter, that butcher with a chisel! Michelangelo? Michel Diavolo! He stabs me in the back, he slanders me, insults me in the street. *Pazzo!* A crazy man! Let him go carve tombstones, that's all he's good for.

"And that simpering, beardless boy Raphael, gawking around trying to copy me. His pictures? They give me a toothache. He should paint with sugar water."

"Pay him no mind," The Gawgon whispered to me as Leonardo ranted. "That's how artists talk about each other."

To draw Leonardo's attention from his colleagues, The Gawgon turned the conversation to his own work. I dared a glance at the sheet of paper on his table, eager to see what brilliant new masterpiece the greatest genius in the world had been pondering.

The page was covered with tic-tac-toe games. Leonardo had been playing against himself and losing.

"I promised Isabella d'Este a painting. Still not begun." Leonardo pulled at his beard. "The town wants a war memorial, a battle scene to cover a church wall. I tore up my sketches. I wanted to do a bronze horse, the biggest ever cast. I haven't even begun the model.

"I don't need this aggravation." Leonardo paced back and forth. "I'll go into some other line of work. I can build fortifications, sewer systems—"

"Did you ever make a cootie-catcher?" I asked.

"I invented it," Leonardo said. He went on with his grumbling. "Earn my bread? Worse comes to worst, I can always play the lute in taverns.

"Painting? No more." Leonardo seized a brush and snapped it in two. "I give it up. *Finito!*"

17

La Gioconda

Leonardo cast around for something else he could break. He snatched up a palette and tried to snap it over his knee. When he did not succeed, he threw it across the studio, where it went sailing into a wall, leaving messy paint stains.

"Stop that nonsense," ordered The Gawgon. "What's the matter with you? What are you telling me, giving up painting? Ridiculous!"

"I've lost my knack." Leonardo's shoulders slumped. "I was doing a portrait. I can't finish it."

"Of course you can," said The Gawgon. "A simple picture? You could dash it off with your left hand."

"I *am* left-handed," Leonardo retorted.

"I forgot," said The Gawgon. "All right, you could do it in your sleep."

"Not this one. Besides, who sleeps? I haven't had a decent night since I started this disaster. You want to know?"

"I'm sure you'll tell us," said The Gawgon.

"All right, if you insist," Leonardo said. "I'm here in the studio, going about my business. I'm thinking of my bronze horse. How to cast it? Interesting technical problem, it would have to be in sections. Yes, and that *pazzo* Michelangelo got wind of the project. He mocked me, right in the middle of the piazza. He said I didn't have the nerve, the gall to try anything so colossal—"

"Enough horse, enough Michelangelo," said The Gawgon. "Then what?"

"So, I'm sitting doing calculations for the molds when in walks a puffed-up idiot. I knew of him: Francesco del Giocondo, retired with a fortune, money pouring out his ears, but a miser nonetheless. He just got married, he wants a portrait of his wife—his third. The first two must have died to escape him; it would have been a pleasure for them. The new one didn't have a ducat of her own, no dowry, no property. Why did such a skinflint bother with her?

"Anyway, I tell him I have better things to do. 'Go ask Raphael,' I say. 'He'll make her look like an angel and do it on the cheap.'

"But that won't answer. It has to be me, no other. He takes out a purse and jingles it under my nose. He's talking cash, gold, a lot of it."

"And you agreed," said The Gawgon.

"What else?" Leonardo shrugged. "An artist has to live. 'Good,' he says. 'Only the best for my little Lisa. You make a nice picture. Understand?'

"Next day, he brings her to the studio. My eyes popped. I see why he didn't care if she had no dowry. *Bellissima!* Beautiful, you can't believe. She's, what, twenty something? And married to that ancient goat? Ah, well, I tell myself, this is Florence and what's a poor girl to do?

"She sits calm and relaxed, very sure of herself, no wiggling, no complaining she's getting a stiff neck. Only the best for little Lisa? Who could do less? I was inspired, I began to work. It went well, so easily. Then—catastrophe!"

"What happened?" asked The Gawgon as Leonardo paused to sigh.

"She smiled," he said.

"So?" said The Gawgon. "Everybody smiles when they have their portrait painted."

"Not like she did," Leonardo said. "She knows secrets, past anything I could understand. Little Lisa? No, with that smile she's every woman in the world, every woman since time began. I had to catch her smile; my life depended on it.

"I couldn't. She never smiled that way again. I try everything to bring it back. I recite poems to her, pile flowers in the studio, sprinkle perfume. I have musicians come and play. No use. I think she's teasing, daring me to make her do it.

"For how long?" Leonardo spread a hand and counted the fingers. "Three, four, five—"

"Who paints a portrait in less than a week?" The Gawgon broke in. "Not even you. Give it a few more days."

"Not days! Years!" cried Leonardo. "Close to six years I'm working on it. I put everything else aside, turned down commissions, gave up my bronze horse."

Leonardo stamped over to the easel and pulled away a sheet covering his painting. "*Ecco!* Defeat! Ruination!"

The Gawgon stared, hardly breathing. I did the same. Leonardo had worked mostly in rich, dark tones. In the background, the landscape alone was a masterpiece; it looked as if it had come out of a dream. But it was the figure itself that so bewitched us. Lisa sat quietly, hands at rest, without rings, bracelets, or any other jewelry, in the simplest of gowns; the most miraculous picture I had ever seen.

Only one thing was missing: her face.

Not entirely. To be more accurate, Leonardo had finished everything but the lips. It was all there except the smile.

"See what I mean?" Leonardo burst out. "Hopeless!"

The Gawgon had stepped a little away from the easel. She stood silently, lost in her own thoughts, on her features a mysterious look I had never seen until this moment.

Leonardo was glooming around and muttering to himself. I took his arm and pointed at The Gawgon.

"Is that the kind of smile you were talking about?" I said.

Leonardo stared at her. His jaw dropped, he nearly fell over backward. He ran to get the palette he had flung against the wall, snatched a new brush, and began working like a madman, all the while yelling at The Gawgon to hold her expression and not to move a muscle.

It did not take him long—after all, he was a genius. When he finished, he tossed brush and palette in the air and capered around the studio.

"That's it! At last!" he cried. "All right, you can move now."

The Gawgon went to study the finished portrait. "Yes, Leo, you've pulled off another miracle as usual. Lisa won't notice somebody else smiled for her. Or, what's the difference? Women all know the same things and smile the same way over them. So, it's done. You can deliver it only six years late—"

"Deliver what?" Leonardo protectively spread his arms. "Deliver nothing! *Niente!* I'm keeping her for myself.

"I'm leaving town," he added. "Enough of Florence. Lisa's coming with me. I still have a few little touch-ups to do."

"Somehow, Leo," said The Gawgon, "I'm not surprised."

"Good luck with the big horse," I said.

━━━━━━━━━━━━━━ **Thuh End** ━━━━━━━━━━━━━━

My twelfth birthday came at the worst of a Philadelphia winter. We were housebound, ice coated Lorimer Street, snow drifted into the areaway and back alley. My father tied his derby to his head with a muffler, armed himself with a coal shovel, and made threatening gestures at the drifts. My mother took over and did a little better, but finally gave up. I volunteered—Admiral Peary hacking his way to the North Pole—but my offer was declined. Deprived of her Tulip Garden, my sister moped in her room and did not volunteer at all.

"God put it there," my father said. "Let Him take it away."

"Oh, Alan," my mother said, "you shouldn't talk like that. He might hear you."

Instead of the usual birthday party with my aunts and grandmother, there were only the four of us. My mother baked a cake, as she always did; I blew out the candles in one breath, as I always did. For gifts, I received handkerchiefs and underwear.

My father, all that week, did not go in town. He left the store closed and did not worry about business. There had not been enough business to worry about since his failed hopes with the Mexican jumping beans. The beans themselves had stopped twitching altogether. He told my mother to throw them out.

"Certainly not," she said. "They'll be all right. They're hibernating."

My sister was kept home from school, although given the equipment, I believe she would have hitched a sled to a team of huskies and mushed her way to rejoin the Tulip Garden. As far as I was concerned, I might as well have been quarantined without the distinction of a Board of Health sticker on the front door.

Lessons with The Gawgon had to be suspended. Even after the weather cleared, I did not go to see her. My grandmother had telephoned, saying it was better to put things off a little while. I stayed in my room and drew pictures of Leonardo tramping along the roads, with a sack tied to the end of a pole and the *Mona Lisa* tucked under his arm. In the distance, Michelangelo flung Italian gestures at him.

It was another week before I went to Larchmont Street. My mother walked with me. The sun had come out bright enough to blind us. It was almost warm.

"Don't stay long," my mother told me. She, Aunt Florry, and my grandmother talked in the kitchen. I went upstairs.

The Gawgon was in bed, sitting up with her back propped against some pillows, the flannel bathrobe wrapped around her. The curtains had been pulled back to let in a big shaft of sunlight with motes dancing in it.

"Happy birthday, Boy." The Gawgon looked in good spirits, so I knew Dr. McKelvie had not been there today. "Better late than never. What's that you have?"

I had brought my drawings of Leonardo and the *Mona Lisa.* I handed them to her. "You can keep them if you want."

The Gawgon laughed and said, "Heaven help us, what will you think of next? I have something for you, too. On the desk."

I picked up the package and tore off the wrapping paper. She had given me a treasure: the second of the three-volume set of history books.

"When you've chewed through that," she said, "you'll be ready for the third. I'll save it for an Easter present."

Hardly able to take my eyes off the book, I waited for her to start our lesson. She seemed content to scan the drawings.

"You've got a little better at it," she said, "but you still need to look harder at things. What I'm thinking," she went on, "suppose we go to the park. Not now. When it's warm enough so we won't freeze. Try sketching from life—the trees, pigeons, people sitting on benches. It might do you good."

I offered my own sudden inspiration. I could draw The Gawgon's portrait. That, I said, would be sketching from life. As a further inducement, I told her I could put the Pyramids in the background; she could be sitting on one of them, the way she did when she was a girl.

"I dread to think how I'd come out now." The Gawgon chuckled. "That would be quite a sight. We'll see, we'll see. All right, then. You can start tomorrow."

She leaned back her head. I understood she wanted me to go. I thanked her again for the book. When I left, she was smiling at the pictures in her hands.

The Gawgon died in her sleep that night.

18

The Legatee

"I think," my father said to my mother, "you'd better take him home."

My mother nodded. She put an arm around my shoulders and led me into a dim corridor so deeply carpeted our footsteps made no sound. She sat beside me on a hard-cushioned sofa that smelled of disinfectant. I knew I had behaved badly.

We were, that afternoon, in J. Robert Rockamore & Sons funeral parlor, a tall building in center city between a travel agency and a ladies' dress salon. All the rich and fashionable dead went to Rockamore's. Not that we counted among them, but Uncle Eustace managed to get us squeezed in. He knew people there, professional courtesy was involved. Not only was he supplying the tombstone at cost, he had also worked out some kind of cut-rate transaction. He was proud of his accomplishment.

"It wasn't easy," Uncle Eustace said. "They have a waiting list."

I had never been to a funeral, let alone to Rockamore's. We entered the lobby through a pair of massive bronze doors sculpted with acanthus leaves and twisted vines. That, I thought, was what the gates of Hell must look like. Inside, Egyptian-style lamps stood on pedestals. The elevator, also with bronze doors, hissed gently as the operator took us to the top floor. No one spoke to him, but he evidently knew where we were supposed to go.

The parlor, one of Rockamore's smallest, seemed a little cramped. Since we did not have enough men in the family, Uncle Eustace had to pay extra for pallbearers. They took up as much space as we did. They stood mute against the wall, six broad-shouldered young men glad for part-time work, black-suited, white-gloved hands clasped over their groins—a posture I would see in later life taken by wedding ushers and politicians on solemn occasions.

Though Uncle Eustace had not contracted for an organist, strains leaked out from someone else's parlor down the hall, and we had the benefit of secondhand music free of charge.

Our vicar, Mr. Granville, was there to conduct the ceremony. Uncle Eustace had first thought to scout around for a Presbyterian.

"That's what she was," he said.

Aunt Rosie put her foot down. "No, Eustace, that just won't do. We can't have some stranger coming in and mumbling who knows what kind of prayers. No, she'll have to go as an Episcopalian."

My mother and aunts were in the same sad dresses they wore for Mrs. Jossbegger. My sister and I had no official mourning costumes, so we made do with Sunday best. There was one basket of flowers from all of us.

Mr. Granville, at some point, made a gesture and we lined up. I had no idea what we were supposed to do. I saw my grandmother bend over and kiss the figure in the casket; then, one by one, the rest of us followed.

When my turn came, I could not do it. I broke away, choking and crying. I knew, shamefully, I was making a scene.

That was when my mother took me into the hall, where I quieted a little. After a time, Mr. Granville appeared in his white cassock, the pallbearers following with the casket, and I started up all over again.

There was some quick conversation between my mother and father. The upshot: I should not go to the graveside. My mother agreed she would have to take me home, which she did.

I was sick to my stomach but thankful I had not thrown up at Rockamore's. My mother put me to bed and gave me some tea. I tossed and turned and finally dozed off.

The night-light was on when I opened my eyes. It must

have been late; the house was quiet. I raised my head, more asleep than awake. In a corner of the room, I saw a rocking chair.

The Gawgon was sitting in it.

"You didn't kiss me good-bye," she said.

"I couldn't," I said. "It wasn't you."

"Quite right," she agreed. "It wasn't."

"Are you a ghost?" I said. "A duppy?"

"Of course not."

"But—but," I said, "what are you? Where did you go after—"

"Nowhere. I never went away from you. Did you suppose I would?"

I did not know what to answer.

"I'm in your imagination," The Gawgon said. "You're making me up as you go along."

"Then," I finally said, "you're all right?"

"Yes, I'm all right," The Gawgon said. "And so are you."

"That's good," I said. "I'm glad."

The Gawgon was still watching me as I turned over and went peacefully to sleep.

The following Sunday afternoon, Uncle Rob and Aunt Rosie stopped by. They brought some cardboard cartons and shoe boxes into the dining room and put them on the table. Uncle Rob's face had the same official look as when he carved turkey, so I assumed adult business matters were involved. It surprised me when Uncle Rob motioned for me to sit with them.

"Annie made a will. Did you know that?" he said, more to my mother and father than to me. "I'd been at her for years, but she kept putting it off. Well, a few weeks ago she got around to it."

"Why, for heaven's sake, did she bother?" Aunt Rosie said. "She had nothing to leave anybody."

Uncle Rob, meantime, had tucked up his sleeves and consulted figures on a piece of paper. There were, he said, some stocks and bonds, but the companies had gone bankrupt. There was a savings account, not enough to cover expenses. He calculated everyone would have to chip in to make up the difference when Rockamore's bill came. The few pieces of furniture in her room might as well stay there; no one would buy them, and they would be useful when the room got rented out.

"Now, you, Skinamalink." Uncle Rob finally spoke directly to me. He waved a hand at the boxes. "These are yours. That's what the will says."

"Well, well, Bax," my father said, "you're a legatee."

I asked if I could open the boxes. Uncle Rob nodded:

"They're yours, you can do anything you want with them."

The first thing I saw when I opened one of the lids was the third of the three-volume history; under it, Shakespeare's plays; a thick, gilt-edged anthology of poems; some Sherlock Holmes; the drawings I had given her at Christmas and the last ones of Leonardo and Michelangelo. In the shoe box were postcards of famous paintings; snapshots of her son; the photo of the Pyramids and The Gawgon with her girl's bright face.

These were treasures beyond any I could have imagined. I thought I had better take the boxes to my room, where I could look into them privately. I began hauling them upstairs.

"Just what I meant," Aunt Rosie was saying. "Poor dear, she had nothing."

My father, that spring, seldom went in town to the store. I stayed mostly in my room. I had no heart to read the books or draw pictures. The tangled yarn lay untouched on the night table. I felt bad that I had not undone more knots. The Gawgon would have been disappointed in me, as I was disappointed in myself.

No one said anything about another teacher. I did not ask. Several times a week, my mother visited my grandmother. I went along and talked to Nora, but without much enthusiasm.

The Gawgon's room had been rented to someone named Mr. Vance. I saw him once or twice: a tight-faced man who wore wing-tip shoes. Uncle Eustace had somewhere struck up an acquaintance and recommended Mr. Vance as a reliable lodger. Men in dark overcoats and gray felt hats often came to visit him, carrying packages in and out. His door was usually closed.

My grandmother occasionally received penny postcards from Uncle Will. He was living in a boardinghouse in Detroit and, miraculously, had found part-time work in a factory.

"He sounds happy. He deserves to be." My grandmother studied his latest message. "It seems he has a lady friend."

"He writes that on a postcard?" exclaimed Aunt Rosie, who was there when the news arrived. "Where the mailman and anybody else can read it?"

"I'm sure the mailman isn't interested," my grandmother said.

Aunt Rosie snorted. "I'm sure he is."

Going down the hall one evening, I saw my sister's door was open and the light on. She was sitting on the edge of her bed. Neck bent, shoulders drooping, she looked so forlorn and miserable I thought she might have broken a fingernail. I stood a few moments in the doorway. When she noticed me, she did not yell at me to go away. This was extraordinary. I ventured in and asked what was wrong.

"I'm not going to Rittenhouse Academy anymore," she said.

That, I said, was wonderful news. I congratulated her on being so lucky.

"You stupid blighter," she said, "I'm not going back and neither are you. Never."

That was a happy relief. I had feared, without someone to give me lessons, I might be returned to the clutches of Dr. Legg. I had planned, if such a disaster threatened, on trumping up some new and horrible sickness.

"Didn't they tell you?" she said.

Generally speaking, no one told me anything right away. If it was important, they would get around to it sooner or later.

"Father's closing the store," she said. "He's selling our house. Grandmother's, too."

At first, I wondered if she was just making it up to torment me, but she looked so awful she had to be sincere. Still, it made no sense. Where would we live?

"We're moving," she said. "Grandmother and Aunt Florry, too. Father bought a new house.

"Don't you understand?" she flung at me. "We have to go away. All of us. To some stupid place."

I was so dumbstruck I sat down beside her. She had, thus far, been speaking bitterly and resentfully. Now she started crying. So did I. We actually put our arms around each other.

19

The Irish Shillelly

My sister's information about unpleasant things was, as always, right. By the time my parents got around to telling me, it came as no surprise. Late that spring, with my grandmother, Aunt Florry, and Nora, we moved to a place called Rosetree Hill, a dozen or so miles from Philadelphia.

We called it the new house, but it was a very old one. It stood at the far end of Lakeview Avenue. Though I saw no lake to view, I learned there had been one, filled in when the neighborhood was built up. There were reminders of its presence when it seeped through the cellar floor, setting the basement awash at regular intervals.

"It looks like the Ming Dynasty," said my father, standing in the middle of the living room after everything was installed. He had closed his store and sold the contents, salvaging as much as he could in the way of lamps, screens, wall hangings, and some lacquered tables. The effect was definitely Oriental. The Mexican jumping beans had been lost in the shuffle.

I never understood my father's business dealings. I could only guess he had sold or rented out the houses on Lorimer Street and Larchmont Street, calculating we could live on that money until he went into a new business.

He had bought the house as soon as he saw it. Dirt cheap, he said. Understandably, for it was falling apart. The faucets dripped with continuous tinklings, like wind chimes. The floors sagged, the plumbing moaned and gargled when anyone flushed the toilet. The stairs sloped at an acute angle, strenuous to climb up, perilous to climb down.

"It's a fine house," my father said. "You won't find another like it."

"I'm sure not," my mother said.

"Now, that's what I call a property." My father held out his arms in an all-embracing gesture. "Land."

What he meant was the house had a front lawn. It was covered with bald spots as if the grass had a skin disease. Instead of an alley and areaway, there was an equally afflicted yard in the back, where sturdy clumps of weeds flourished. A porch and wooden railing ran along the front of the house. Chains dangled from the porch ceiling where once had been a swing. They looked like equipment from a medieval torture chamber.

It was the last house on Lakeview Avenue. Farther down were vacant lots. Still farther, at the dead end, some woods began: spindly trees and thickets. Our neighbors' neatly trimmed lawns seemed to pull their skirts away from us, leaving our property to itself in a sort of real-estate Hell.

My father was proud of the new house. I hated it.

If my grandmother's boardinghouse expanded and contracted like an accordion, our new house was more like a rabbit warren, with closets, cubbyholes, a pantry with lopsided shelves. Nora, with her cage and pole, held pride of place in the Ming Dynasty living room. We had not enough bedrooms to go 'round, so I was assigned to the attic—partly finished, it was called, which meant that one side was bandaged with wallpaper; the other, a skeleton of rafters. I was warned never to walk on the area in front of the eaves or I would crash through to the floor below.

I tossed and turned most of our first night in the new house. My old familiar bed felt as if we had never met. I had no idea what time it was when I woke again.

The Gawgon was sitting on my unpacked boxes.

I was surprised but happy to see her. "We moved," I said. "How did you find the house?"

"I can always find you," The Gawgon said.

I blurted out that I hated the place.

"Understandable," she said. "Nobody likes being uprooted. You'll get used to it."

I said I doubted that.

"Where's your imagination, Boy?" she answered. "You can

turn this house into anything you please. King Arthur's castle, if
you like. Or Dracula's, with bats and a vampire's coffin in the
cellar.

"Or a Parisian garret," she went on, "with starving artists
running in and out. A beautiful model having her picture
painted—you're old enough to be interested in that sort of
thing."

I began cheering up. Before The Gawgon could continue, I
heard doors banging open and my father yelling. I jumped out
of bed and stumbled down the attic steps.

Everybody was awake. My father, in striped pajamas, was
heading for the landing, my mother behind him, telling him to
put on his bedroom slippers.

"Nobody move! Stand where you are!" my father commanded. "I've got a gun!"

Sleep-fuddled and confused, I called out the first thing that
came to mind:

"Don't shoot The Gawgon!"

"Oh, Alan, you don't have a gun," my mother said. "If anybody's there, why tell them to stay?"

My father paid no attention. He was waving his arms and
hurrying down the stairs while my mother tried to hold him
back. He managed the first couple of steps, but lost his footing
and went skidding down the rest. It brought him to the living
room faster than if he had walked.

All the lights were on by now. We clattered after him. Unruffled by his rapid descent, he inspected the living room. He

was sure, he said, he heard prowlers. He found none and stepped through the dining room into the kitchen.

The cupboard was open, so was the icebox. The latch on the pantry door had been broken. A cracked egg lay on the linoleum floor.

"Burglars," my father said. "I told you so."

My grandmother and Aunt Florry came to look around the kitchen while my sister observed from a distance. My mother surveyed the shelves and icebox. Missing, along with our eggs, were bottles of milk, some pork chops, a box of cornflakes, sugar, coffee, and a bag of flour.

"They only took the food. They didn't touch anything else," my mother said. "God help them, that's all they wanted."

She sat down at the table and began to cry.

Aunt Florry and my grandmother tidied up. My father toured the backyard to see if the burglars were hiding amid the weeds.

I went back to the attic. The Gawgon was not there.

"What we really need," my father announced, "is a tree."

"Oh, Alan," my mother said, "whatever for?"

"Landscaping." My father stood on the front porch and surveyed the property. He narrowed his eyes as if scanning a vast expanse. "We need one"—he pointed at a bare spot in the middle of the lawn—"right there."

When my mother asked where he expected to get a tree, he

motioned beyond the vacant lot at the end of Lakeview Avenue. "In the woods."

"Steal one?" my mother said.

"Who'll notice?" Without further discussion, he formed us into a raiding party. He walked ahead, as pioneer and pathfinder; I followed, carrying a spade salvaged from a heap of rusty tools abandoned in the cellar. My mother, holding a burlap sack, brought up the rear.

In the woods—I had begun thinking of it as Sherwood Forest—the only trees he liked were too big to dig up. He had to settle for a tormented-looking sapling with skinny branches and barely any leaves. None of us knew what kind; my father said it didn't matter. We wrapped the straggly roots in the sack. He carried it like a baby in his arms. At the house, he called out for my grandmother, Aunt Florry, and my sister. We took turns excavating a hole. Then he went inside and came back with a pair of scissors.

"For good luck." He ceremoniously snipped locks of hair from everyone's head, including his own. He laid them, with one of Nora's feathers, in the bottom of the hole.

"We can plant it now," he said. "It's our family tree."

Later in the afternoon, Aunt Rosie and Uncle Rob drove out to see how we were getting on. Aunt Rosie stared at the addition to the yard:

"What, for heaven's sake, do you call that?"

"I call it a tree," my father retorted.

"What's that crookedy stick the Irish carry to hit each other?" Aunt Rosie asked Uncle Rob.

"A shillelagh," he said.

"That's it," Aunt Rosie said. "It looks like an Irish shillelly."

We all went to the porch, where my father had us stand to get a better perspective on the sapling. If we squinted a little, he said, we could see traces of green.

A dog, just then, came wandering past the house and sighted our family tree. Wagging his tail, an eager grin on his face, he trotted up and peed on it.

Each day after that, dogs of every size and ancestry showed up. Some I did not recognize as belonging in the neighborhood; they must have traveled from miles away, all members of a widespread network, a peeing society with its meeting place at the Irish shillelly—its permanent name, thanks to Aunt Rosie. We chased them off whenever we saw them.

My father did not worry about the dogs. The Irish shillelly showed signs of actually growing a little. As my father saw it, we were getting free fertilizer.

20

A Swimming Party

I nearly drowned, that summer, and also fell in love. The drowning part came first, but both events happened at practically the same time. I very sensibly did not mention either one to my family.

In any case, they were all occupied with other things. Now that we had settled into the new house, my father concentrated on making a living. He thought about it a lot, mainly while sitting on the porch, eyes closed in meditation, sometimes glancing up to admire the Irish shillelly. He still read the financial pages of the newspaper, more out of habit than anything else, for there were no finances to read about.

"All in due course, all in due course," he assured my mother when she asked what he had in mind. "I'm planning my strategy."

Aunt Florry, it turned out, was the first to get a real job. Her old employer, Mrs. Heberton, had been as good as her word. She did ask around on Aunt Florry's behalf. Through her influence, Aunt Florry was hired as a clerk in the mortgage department of the biggest bank in Philadelphia. Always a nifty dresser, she looked especially nifty when, each morning, she walked the quarter mile to the trolley. Not only an old and most distinguished institution, the bank also provided free lunches to its employees. When she came home in the evening, Aunt Florry often brought some buttered rolls, a slice of pie, or other portable tidbits saved out of her meal and wrapped in paper napkins.

My grandmother had news from Uncle Will. Instead of a postcard, this time he wrote a letter, saying he was getting married.

"I'm glad," my grandmother said. "I only hope she treats him better than"—she rolled her eyes—"you know who."

I did not, but everyone else did. All agreed it was a good thing for Uncle Will, so I was happy for him.

My sister was too busy to pay much attention to any of that. She cultivated another Tulip Garden.

Our first week or two in Rosetree Hill, she had been sullen and brooding. Then, almost overnight, a Tulip Garden sprang up. I never learned whether she grew a new one or got transplanted into one already flowering; nor did I understand how she managed it so quickly. But all at once, there they were,

looking the same as the previous group though noticeably blos-
somed out.

On hot afternoons, they clustered, long-legged in their
summer frocks, in languid attitudes on the porch steps. Most of
the time, along with the standard whispering and giggling, they
gossiped about the young men of Rosetree Hill; in particular,
someone called Nick Ormond. The very name carried enough
magical power to send them swooning in rapture. Nick Ormond, I gathered, was the local hero. Like my sister and her
companion tulips, he was going to be a senior at Rosetree High
School that coming fall. A foregone conclusion, beyond any
doubt, he would be captain of the football team, head of the
student council, class president, and, later, king of the world.

As with the previous Tulip Garden, their company was forbidden to me.

"Make him keep away," my sister warned them. "He'll try
to look down your dress."

This was true, but I thought nobody noticed. And so I
could only ogle and eavesdrop from a distance.

My father, meanwhile, had struck on a plan to make a fortune.

"The River Jordan," he said. "I'm going to buy it."

"Oh, Alan, that's ridiculous," my mother said. "I'm sure it's
not for sale."

"Not the whole river," my father said. "Just some."

His plan involved importing Jordan water by the barrel. He

would then repackage it in small bottles, like perfume, and sell them—along with a fancy certificate—for baptisms. The Jordan water would get babies off to a good start in life.

He proposed using regular tap water and adding a few drops from the Jordan.

"A little," he said, "should go a long way."

My mother wanted no part of the scheme. Diluting water with water, even Jordan water, seemed dishonest. And who knew what kind of trouble he could get himself into, especially with God Almighty?

My father said he would take his chances, we needed the money. Since he was unsure who actually owned the river and how he might buy some from a spot nobody cared about, he wrote letters to kings, prime ministers, and various ambassadors. Awaiting their answers, he went back to studying the financial pages.

For myself, idle, I scuffed around the house and halfheartedly chased dogs away from the shillelly, which persisted in putting out a couple of leaves from time to time. Most often, I holed up in the attic with The Gawgon's books.

The Gawgon still came to visit, although irregularly. Once, poking at the clutter on my table, she gave me a quizzical look:

"What, Boy, you've stopped drawing pictures?"

I nodded. I had, indeed, given that up; nor had I bothered to think of any foolish stories. I told her I hadn't felt like it.

"As good a reason as any," The Gawgon said. "You'll start again, sooner or later."

No, I said. Things weren't the same.

"Nothing stays the same," The Gawgon said. "Not you, not anything else. Don't worry, you'll find what you need."

"I don't care," I said.

The Gawgon left. I was sorry. It was the first time I had been any way snappish to her.

Occasionally, for the sake of getting away from the house, I wandered the neighborhood, hoping to find boys my own age. The only ones in the vicinity were several years older than I. They were cordial enough; they simply had their own interests.

I ventured, one day, past the end of the street, beyond Sherwood Forest, where it turned into serious woods, thick with trees and heavy underbrush, outcroppings of rocks, gullies that fell away so suddenly I nearly tumbled into them. I pressed on and soon came to a creek bubbling over a stony bed.

I followed it a while. Farther along, I heard whoops and yells. The creek had widened into a modest river with sloping, pebbly banks. Half a dozen older boys were swimming, splashing, and ducking each other with a lot of merriment and horseplay.

I picked my way closer to stand and watch. They noticed me but neither chased me away nor invited me to join them. One, sandy-haired, with a pair of athletic legs and black swim trunks, was clearly the leader. When he jumped into the water, so did everyone else; when he sunned himself on the shore, they all squatted around him.

Had my sister been there, she would have gone berserk, for one of his entourage addressed him as "Nick." It dawned on me I was in the very presence of that paragon of animals and future king of the world: Nick Ormond himself.

I hung around the fringe of this activity for a time. When they tired of swimming, they all traipsed off together and left the creek to me. It looked so inviting, with the sunlight flashing on the green ripples, I thought how pleasant it would be to go for a swim. I glanced around, making sure I was unobserved, then peeled down to my underwear.

The water, when I stepped into it, was chillier than I expected; gooseflesh erupted all over me. I got used to it after a minute or so, and launched myself into the current.

There were only two difficulties. First, I had never been in water this deep; second, I did not know how to swim.

These had not seemed insurmountable problems. I had watched Nick and his friends. It looked simple and easy enough. I followed their example. And sank like a stone. By the time I realized I should have kept my mouth shut, I believed I had swallowed half the creek while the other half poured up my nose and into my ears. I thrashed around, which only made matters worse. I assumed I was drowning, and that could get me in serious trouble at home.

In the course of kicking and flailing, and yelling when I

found enough breath to do it, my feet scraped the bottom. It occurred to me, in some dim instinct for survival, to stand up. When I did, the water came barely to my shoulders. All I had to do was walk out. Gasping and coughing, I lumbered against the current, which felt like crawling through molasses. Torn between gratitude for my salvation and fury at my idiocy, I sprawled on the bank.

After a few minutes, I put my clothes on. My head pounded; water filled my ears and made fluttering noises as if moths had nested there. I still shook, frightened and freezing. I thought I had better go home.

As a shrewd and canny woodsman, I followed the creek in the direction I had come from. I had, by then, dried out, warmed up, and started feeling pleased at my conduct. The creek, in my adjusted recollection, became much wider and swifter, with high waves and a treacherous undertow. I had dealt with it well.

Busy congratulating myself, I must have made a wrong turn. Instead of reaching Lakeview Avenue, I found myself deeper in the woods. I recognized nothing familiar. The faster I walked, I reckoned, the sooner I would be out of the place, which had begun looking suddenly weird and sinister. This led me nowhere. I had to admit I was hopelessly lost, never to be seen again until someone eventually tripped over my skeleton. The most sensible reaction was blind panic. I went scrambling straight through the underbrush.

21

My Sweet Gloria

Euclid claimed, as The Gawgon taught me, the shortest distance between two points was a straight line. I was not able to apply that principle. I kept zigzagging as brambles maliciously sprang up and got in the way. I lost track of where I had been and where I was trying to go. I did, soon, come to a dirt road. A stone bridge spanned the creek, which had either looped back on itself or I had been running around in a circle. Lacking any better idea, I crossed over it. After a dozen more yards, the woods ended and I burst through into civilization.

This was a part of Rosetree Hill I had never seen before: large, handsome houses, tall trees lining both sides of the street. I headed for the nearest house, hoping to find other human beings.

What I found was Nick Ormond. Still in his black trunks,

the future king of the world was pushing a lawn mower. I dared to approach. I called to him by name. This did not surprise him. He may have recognized me from the creek; perhaps he took for granted that everybody knew him. He stopped mowing the grass—I hardly believed the paragon of animals was doing such a humble chore—and looked me up and down. I tried to be properly respectful, all the while wondering how to ask directions without shamefully confessing I was lost. I told him my name and where I lived.

"Don't you have a sister?" he asked, before I could get around to my own questions. "Elise?"

Amazed that he was aware of her existence, I admitted I did. He nodded and grew almost cordial. I hinted I was on my way to Lakeview Avenue, wherever that might be.

Meantime, a substantial, silver-haired man with a neatly trimmed mustache had come from behind the house. He wore white duck pants and a short-sleeved shirt with crossed golf clubs embroidered on the breast pocket. Nick, who seemed to know we had just moved into the neighborhood, told him who I was, adding a mention of my sister.

The man—Nick's father—courteously shook my hand. "Lakeview Avenue? Well, son, you've got yourself all mixed up." He eyed the scratches on my arms and legs. "Been hacking around the woods? They can fool you if you don't know them."

He turned to Nick. "Ready for lemonade?" Nick declared he surely was. The two started down the driveway. Mr. Ormond glanced back. "Come on, you have some, too. I think you could use a good stiff drink." He laughed good-naturedly. "Nonalcoholic, of course."

I accepted gratefully. I followed them down a driveway to a big backyard lined with flower beds. Nick went and stretched out in a hammock slung between two trees. Mr. Ormond motioned for me to sit on a wooden bench at a trestle table. Mrs. Ormond, a pleasant-looking woman of my mother's age, came out the back door. She brought a tray with tall glasses and a chrome-plated ice bucket. Beside her, carrying a pitcher, walked a slender girl in a sundress.

"We need another glass, my dear," Mr. Ormond said to the girl. "We have an unexpected guest."

With a curious glance at me, she disappeared into the house. By the time she came back, Mrs. Ormond had taken up a pair of tongs and dropped ice into the tumblers. Mr. Ormond made brief introductions as Mrs. Ormond poured out the lemonade. Gloria, so their daughter was named, turned closer attention on me. Whereas her brother's hair was close-cropped and yellowish, hers was golden brown, long, with lighter streaks in it. She had wide-set, blue-green eyes, and they made me ill at ease, for she seemed to be studying me with secret amusement.

"Hey, sis, where's mine?" Nick, without raising himself from the hammock, held out an arm and wiggled his fingers. "Bring it here, twit."

"Lazy lump," Gloria called back. "Get it yourself."

Nick made a great show of protesting he was tired, ordering her to be a good little brat and do as she was told, and they tossed insults back and forth. Mr. and Mrs. Ormond, evidently used to this, paid them no mind.

Gloria sighed and shrugged. With a wicked little curve to her lips, she went to the hammock. Instead of putting the glass in Nick's hand, she poured the contents, ice and all, onto his head. Nick, roaring, tipped himself out of the hammock and sprawled full-length on the grass. He started after his sister, on her smiling way to the table.

"Enough. Stop it," Mrs. Ormond said. "No more nonsense, either of you. We have company."

Nick refilled his glass, which Gloria had let fall to the ground. He took it to the front yard. He was more than a little vexed; no doubt he had his reputation to uphold in front of strangers.

Gloria, unruffled, sipped her drink, as I did my own. It was nectar of the gods; even the ice was delicious—in glittering cubes, not slivers, which meant the Ormonds had one of the new electric refrigerators. More than all that, Gloria handed me my lemonade with such a graceful motion, and looked full at me over the rim of her tumbler. That was probably when I fell in love with her. People, I suppose, have fallen in love for less reason.

Mr. Ormond, meantime, had been asking about my family, how long we had been in Rosetree Hill, and what my father did. I was reluctant to explain about buying the River Jordan; I only said he imported things. I added that my aunt worked at the biggest bank in town.

"What a coincidence," Mr. Ormond said. "So do I."

It was a pleasant enough conversation until Mrs. Ormond began talking about school, as adults do when they know nothing better to say to children. Gloria, she mentioned, would be going into seventh grade at Rosetree Junior High.

"You look the same age," she added. "I imagine that's where you'll go, too."

Junior high? From what my mother had calculated, I would, in the fall, go to elementary school as a sixth grader.

So besotted with Gloria, I had not given a thought to school and grades. This was monstrous. The elementary school and the junior high were miles apart, geographically and every other way. I knew the ironbound, unbreakable system of class and caste. I had seen and lived it myself at Rittenhouse Academy.

It was unthinkable, unspeakable, maybe illegal, for anyone in a higher grade to have anything but scorn and contempt for anyone in a lower. I could already see Gloria's lovely face fill with horror. Her fond glances—as I was sure they were—would turn to disgust, as if I had been transformed into a slithering reptile, a warty toad, a less than human creature covered with oozing sores and trailing clouds of poisonous dandruff.

Between now and autumn—who knew what might happen? Before being unmasked as a wretched sixth grader, I could be lucky enough to get squashed by a truck.

And so I took the only reasonable course: I lied.

I said I wasn't sure what grade. I had been reading *Tom*

Brown's Schooldays, one of The Gawgon's books, and I grasped at that straw.

"Because, you see," I went on, "it's different in England. They don't have grades, they have forms."

"England?" Mr. Ormond raised an eyebrow.

"To Rugby," I said. "It's a famous school."

I prayed for a thunderbolt to blast me. It did not. I floundered on, explaining that my parents were thinking of sending me there. To assure Gloria our separation would not be long, I added I would be home for the holidays.

"Interesting," said Mr. Ormond. I wondered if he knew I was lying.

"How exciting," said Mrs. Ormond, as if she believed me. "You must be looking forward to it."

Gloria did not comment. I was only looking forward to going home before I dug a deeper pit for myself. I stood up—staggered up, rather, under the burden of my preposterous claim. Mr. Ormond gave me directions to Lakeview Avenue. It was not far, less than a mile; he told me to cross the trolley tracks, turn left there and right someplace else.

I was not keeping any of this straight in my head. I asked him to repeat. Convinced, no doubt, I was an idiot, he finally asked Gloria to take her bicycle and go with me.

"We don't want you getting lost again," Mr. Ormond said.

I was already lost. Gloria went to the garage. I walked down the driveway. Nick Ormond stopped pushing the lawn mower long enough to call, "Say hello to your sister."

Gloria came pedaling into the street. She tossed her long hair and waved for me to follow. I trotted along the pavement, wondering if she meant to make me run all the way. She kept glancing back with the same air of secret amusement she had when we were drinking lemonade, as if teasing me to catch up with her.

Before I lagged too far behind, she circled back, wheeling graceful spirals and figure eights. At last, she dismounted and rolled the bicycle to the pavement. She pushed it along; we walked side by side. She smelled of sunlight and perspiration. She was marvelous.

"We have a parrot," I said.

By then, we had reached Lakeview Avenue. I pointed to our house and asked if she wanted to come in and see Nora. A couple of dogs were sniffing around the Irish shillelly. I chased them away. When I turned back, she was gone.

I had come home just in time for dinner. As we all sat down, my mother looked at me closely and with some concern and asked where I had been all afternoon.

This time I did not lie—except for leaving out the parts about drowning, getting lost in the woods, and falling in love. I offhandedly remarked I had a nice visit with the Ormond family, after happening to run into Nick.

My sister sat bolt upright, as though galvanized by a powerful electric current. I smiled and charitably threw her a crumb.

"Oh," I said, "I almost forgot. Nick was asking for you."

I left her choking and gulping and turned to Aunt Florry. Mr. Ormond, I told her, also worked at her bank.

"He certainly does," Aunt Florry said. "Good heavens, he's a vice president."

My father laughed. "Bax, old sport, you've been hobnobbing with the upper crust."

Aunt Florry reminded us that Mr. Ormond had been her old employer's financial adviser. Mrs. Heberton had spoken to him and recommended her for a job. Everyone was surprised I had been face-to-face with him; underlings at the bank caught only glimpses of Mr. Ormond. They went on to talk about other things.

I ate my dinner quickly and started for the attic. My sister ran after me. I beat her to it and locked the door behind me.

"What did he say?" she yelled. "Exactly."

"I can't remember it all," I said, taking a dumb-ox attitude which she hated. "Something like 'hello to your sister.'"

She squealed and smacked the door as if it were my head. I climbed the rest of the steps to my garret, as I had begun calling it, and flopped on the bed, relishing my thoughts—most of them circling around Gloria. Finally, I rummaged out a sketch pad and soft pencil, meaning to do a portrait of her. I had drawn nothing for such a long time, I could not catch the likeness. I crumpled sheet after sheet and tossed them on the floor.

"Well, Boy, I believe you've gone and lost your heart."

The Gawgon was looking over my shoulder.

I did not answer. I was happy to see her; but I said nothing.

"I'm glad," The Gawgon said. "In fact, I rather hoped you would. Sometimes, the best way to heal a heart is to lose it. But I'm sorry you told such a terrible whopper. It was silly on top of being a lie. Ah, well, it's not the last silly thing you'll ever do."

The Gawgon peered at the sketch I had begun for about the seventeenth time. "That's your little Gloria? Yes, she's a lovely child. It will be a nice portrait."

"I wish I could have drawn yours," I said. "I'm sorry I didn't have the chance. It's not that I haven't been thinking of you. I can still try—"

"No, no," The Gawgon gently said. "We've had our adventures, you and I. Wonderful adventures. I'm glad of them. You go ahead now with your own."

"You don't mind?" I asked. "About Gloria and me?"

"Of course not," The Gawgon said. " 'Summer's lease hath all too short a date.' "

"Shakespeare," I said.

"Correct," said The Gawgon. "Be happy. Good night, Boy."

After breakfast next morning, I went on the porch to stand sentry duty, ready to defend the Irish shillelly. No dogs hove into sight. I was about to climb to my garret and work some more on the portrait. I stopped short. Swift and graceful as an antelope, Gloria came pedaling her bicycle down Lakeview Avenue. She coasted up to the steps.

"You wanted me to see your parrot?" she said.

22

Summer's Lease

Gloria and I were sweethearts that summer. We never talked about it. I wondered if she knew. I believed she did. That was good enough.

We were together from that first morning she came to see Nora. I warned her Nora sometimes nipped, but Gloria went straight to the perch and held out a finger. Nora, charmed, stepped onto it.

She charmed the rest of my family, as well. My mother patted her head and said what a pretty child she was. Gloria had no grandmother. Mine happily substituted, and within a week or two, Gloria was calling her "Grandma Mary."

My sister sweetly fussed over her—Gloria's brother, after all, was king of the world—offering to paint her nails and do her hair. And my sister never called me a stupid blighter—when Gloria was there.

My father was delighted when Gloria oohed and ahhed over the Ming Dynasty living room. Beaming, he explained what all the curios were and where they came from.

"I want to go to China," Gloria said to me later. She had a distant, dreamy look in her eyes. "I want to sail all around the world."

Offering my own adventures on the high seas, I told her I had visited relatives in Jamaica. I made it sound as if the voyage had been marked by hurricanes, threats of shipwreck, and mutiny. I went on about coconuts and mangoes, palm trees and pirate coves.

"Yes," Gloria said. "Oh, yes. I'll go there, too. I'll go everywhere."

If Gloria charmed my family, our house charmed her. She loved the cubbyholes, the Alpine stairway, the wooden icebox with all its doors. She showed tender feelings toward the Irish shillely and helped shoo the dogs away. Our house looked better to me after she had been there. I did come to love it, and loved it, no doubt, because she did.

We saw a lot of each other during those summer days, though I could never be sure when. Gloria would simply show up on her bicycle, or I would walk to the Ormonds' house and hope to find her. Sometimes she was there, sometimes not. I wondered if she kept company with other boys. No, that was too horrible to imagine. I uprooted that idea from my thoughts. But I never knew where she went, and never asked.

My father, meantime, had received no letters from any kings or ambassadors. Annoyed at them, he gave up trying to buy the River Jordan and turned to a brighter prospect.

"Palm-Nutto," he said to my mother. "Diggers wanted me to sell it. He ate some, remember? To show how pure it was."

My father wrote to his boyhood chum in Kingston. In due course, several cases of the household cleanser arrived. Convinced he could sell anything to anybody, he foresaw no difficulties.

His first morning of door-to-door salesmanship, he wore his straw boater with striped hatband and his white summer suit—an ice-cream suit, my mother called it. He stowed a dozen jars in the trunk of our car and drove off with a gnashing of gears.

He came home before noon. He carried his straw hat in his hand, his complexion was a delicate green. No one had bought any. Besides, eating the Palm-Nutto to show its purity made him nauseous. One lady seemed a good prospect but lost interest when he threw up on her floor. He renounced Palm-Nutto then and there.

My mother took over the business and brought home small amounts of cash. She assured my father he was a fine salesman; it was simply that she could talk about housecleaning better than he could. She did not eat any Palm-Nutto.

Uncle Eustace was prospering. While the Depression kept getting worse, his tombstone business kept getting better. It was, he said, thanks to Mr. Vance, who had been a lodger in my grandmother's boardinghouse.

"He's a good sort of fellow, is Vance," Uncle Eustace said. "He never talks about what line of work he's in, but he sends a nice bit of business my way. His friends buy a lot of stones."

"His friends keep shooting each other, if you ask me," my father said. "You're probably selling tombstones to half the gangsters in Philadelphia."

"So?" Uncle Eustace shrugged. "It's a living."

"Gangsters or not, they should have a decent burial," my mother said. "They're just as dead as anybody else."

Gloria, that summer, taught me to ride a bicycle. At her request, Mrs. Ormond let me borrow Nick's outgrown vehicle. It was small for me as well, and I had to be cautious about banging my knees on the handlebars. Gloria never made fun of me when I fell off. Even when I caught the knack of balancing, pedaling, and steering, I never matched her spirals and loops. Still, I could ride to her house quickly; it was a good as having an automobile.

Being in love with her made me shrewd and calculating. I was always afraid she would, one day, glide away on her bicycle and vanish. I kept thinking of schemes to snare her interest.

Not only had I begun studying in earnest, I had also started drawing again. I proposed doing her portrait. That would keep her with me a long time. I would make sure it did. She agreed, and from then on I brought my sketch pad.

My cunning knew no limits. I began a story to be revealed when the time was right. Seeking inspiration, I burglarized Shakespeare from the book The Gawgon left me. Shakespeare had plenty of ideas. He would never notice any missing.

WONDERS OF THE WORLD

*U*nder the cloak of darkness, Davio Aldini strode happily and eagerly to what might cost his life. The clock in the piazza tolled twelve. He quickened his pace and slipped noiselessly through the lavish gardens of the Ormondi estate.

Since that morning in the marketplace, when a street urchin pressed a scrap of paper into his hand, Davio had counted the hours. His heart leaped with joy at the words that could well be his death sentence:

> *My dearest Davio,*
>
> *We must no longer be apart. Come to my chambers at midnight. Second balcony, east wing.*
>
> *Yours truly, and truly yours,*
Gloria Ormondi
>
> *P.S. I'll leave the light on.*

He had glimpsed her only from time to time when the beautiful Gloria and a train of servants bought baskets of lemons for her family's lemonade. Between them, however, passed the melting glances of love at first sight. They had never spoken, nor dared to. The Ormondis and Aldinis, richest and most powerful families in the hill town of Rosamonte, had been mortal enemies for centuries. They had forgotten why but did remember to hate each other.

Davio made his way to the east wing of the Ormondi mansion. Thick greenery covered the wall. A lamp glowed from the chamber casement. He flung aside his cloak nonchalantly as he risked his life and climbed athletically up the vines.

As he was about to swing over the stone balcony, a figure loomed from the shadows.

"My darling!" Davio whispered. "I'm here—"

"And so am I, you sneaking swine!"

Davio stared into the furious face of Mr. Ormondi, whose mustache convulsed with a life of its own.

"You wretch! You dog! You—you Aldini!" roared Mr. Ormondi. "How dare you! What are you up to? Answer me!"

"Aggag," replied Davio, unable to explain further with Mr. Ormondi's hands clamped around his neck. He had resigned himself to death in exchange for a moment with his beloved. He had not reckoned on his tonsils exploding. With all his strength he peeled away Mr. Ormondi's fingers, but, in the desperate struggle, tumbled backward and crashed down through the shrubbery.

Mr. Ormondi bawled for his army of lackeys and retainers. Davio sat up and held his spinning head. He staggered to his feet and lurched away with no clear idea where he was going. A hand seized him by the collar. He flung himself around to face his attacker.

It was Gloria, dressed in the leggings and leather jerkin of a stable-sweeper.

"Quick, my dearest," she urged, while torches flared and angry Ormondis swarmed from the mansion. She hustled the still bewildered Davio through the gardens and into the shadows of the olive trees.

"No time to warn you," Gloria hurried on. "That treacherous little guttersnipe! I shouldn't have trusted him with my letter. He blabbed to my father. I'm sure he was well rewarded."

By now they had reached what looked to Davio like an abandoned toolshed. He stumbled through the door after her. With flint and steel from her jacket, Gloria struck a spark and lit a lamp on the cluttered workbench. Even in her coarse garb and these dilapidated surroundings, she appeared still more radiantly beautiful. He held out his arms to her.

"Alone at last!" cried Davio.

"Not for long," said Gloria. "They'll find us here if we don't get a move on."

"My dearest, we have no escape," Davio said. "But at least we shall spend these final moments together. They will be all the sweeter because of their brevity.

"Then let your father stab me with a bodkin!" Davio snapped his fingers. "I care not a figgo! Let him run me through with a rapier—"

"You?" said Gloria. "And what do you think he'll do to me?"

"We shall have the joy of dying together," Davio pointed out.

"Not a good idea," said Gloria.

She stepped to a corner of the shed where a canvas-draped object leaned against the wall.

"My father's cousin Leo gave him this to try out," Gloria said. "Cousin Leo's a genius at inventing things—and a pretty good artist, too. He only made one of these, then got interested in painting somebody's portrait—Lisa something-or-other—and that was the last we saw of him.

"My father thought it was ridiculous," Gloria went on. "One more of Cousin Leo's harebrained schemes. Useless, my father said. Who'd want it when we have horses?"

Gloria, during this, had untied the cords that secured the canvas and pulled aside the covering. "I think it's wonderful."

Davio blinked at the strange contraption, unlike anything he had seen before. A slender framework had been crafted of polished wood. At the front was what looked like a pair of gracefully curving horns and, at the rear, another pair. Two narrow leather pads had been set on a crossbar. There were two large wooden wheels studded with tiny nailheads.

"Cousin Leo called it a 'velocipedia,' " Gloria said. "I've practiced, I know how it works."

"What's it do?" Davio eyed the machine with mingled curiosity and distrust.

"Gets us away from here." Gloria rolled the velocipedia through the door and motioned for Davio to follow. "The back gate won't be guarded. They're sure an Aldini will be too proud to use the tradesman's entrance."

Gloria was right. They passed quickly through the olive grove and the gate and continued on to a well-paved road. Except for the crowd of vengeful Ormondis, Davio would have enjoyed the moonlit outing with his beloved; but Gloria, after a moment, halted.

"Get on that saddle thing in the back," she directed. "Hold those curved bars. Put your feet on the pedals. I'll do the steering."

Davio did as she instructed. "Now what?"

Gloria swung lightly to the seat in front of him. "Just keep pedaling."

Next thing he knew, the velocipedia shot forward. He found himself pumping like mad as Gloria, likewise pedaling, guided Cousin Leo's vehicle as expertly as the helmsman of a ship. They skimmed along at a breathtaking rate. The wind whistled in Davio's ears. They would have made rapid progress and been well away from Rosamonte if Davio had not lost his balance every few yards and sent himself, Gloria, and the velocipedia into a roadside ditch.

They had picked themselves up for the tenth or twelfth time when Davio, about to remount, paused and cocked his head. From behind them came thundering hoofbeats. Under the moon, in the clear and starlit night, Davio could make out

Mr. Ormondi on horseback, galloping at the front of his retainers, all brandishing pikes and swords.

"Quit staring," ordered Gloria. "Climb back. And keep on pedaling."

For one hopeful instant, Davio believed they might outdistance Mr. Ormondi. His heart sank. Word must have spread like wildfire, for, some distance down the road ahead, galloped his father and every other Aldini in town.

"Trapped between our families!" exclaimed Davio. "All is lost!"

"Keep on pedaling," said Gloria.

From what little he could see, Gloria had taken both hands from her steering bars and begun pulling at several rods and levers.

"I told you Cousin Leo was a genius," she called over her shoulder. "He knew it would take a lot of strength to make this thing go. That's why he made room for two. I never tried this part by myself, but I trust Cousin Leo."

Fearless enough to face a thousand Mr. Ormondis, Davio suddenly felt as if the top of his head were coming off while his terrified stomach sank to his kneecaps. Cleverly folded into the frame of the velocipedia, a pair of light but sturdy wings deployed and flapped steadily. The vehicle began rising. Moments later, it was airborne and rapidly climbing.

"My dearest," cried Davio, "what do we do now?"

"Keep on pedaling," said Gloria.

Below, the galloping Aldinis and Ormondis collided, but instead of hacking and stabbing, they craned their necks skyward in dumbstruck disbelief.

Davio, overcoming his first fear, was developing a taste for soaring into the stars.

"You realize, my darling," he said, "after this, we won't dare go back to Rosamonte."

"Who wants to?" said Gloria. "We'll fly on to China, India, Samoa—"

"What about Jamaica?" Davio said.

"There, too," said Gloria. "Keep on pedaling."

─────────── **Not Thuh End** ───────────

"I like your house better than mine," Gloria said. "At home, it's boring. My father has everything decided ahead of time, all planned out. Nick's going into politics when he gets out of college. It's what my father wants."

We were, that afternoon, sitting on the porch at Lakeview Avenue. I had put down my sketch pad to chase a dog away from the shillelly.

"Nick," Gloria said. "He's my brother and I love him. But he's not nice with girls. He thinks he has—privileges."

We both knew Nick and my sister had been seeing each other. In the end, my sister would have her heart broken. For the moment, she was blissfully happy.

I asked Gloria what her father planned for her.

"He hasn't told me yet." She had the same wicked curve to her lips I saw when she doused her brother with lemonade. "I probably won't like it."

"Then don't do it," I said.

Gloria grinned at me. "I won't." She added, "What are you going to be?"

My answer—I didn't know if it had been stewing in the back of my mind, or, if so, for how long. In any case, it popped out and there it was. I felt as if I had untied one of The Gawgon's knots.

"I'll be an artist," I said. "I'll write stories, too."

Gloria nodded. "You'll be good at that."

I went back to her portrait. I planned, eventually, on adding color as another way of stretching out the project. Gloria asked when it would be finished. I warned her it could take a long time. Leonardo da Vinci, I told her, spent six years on the *Mona Lisa*.

"I don't mind," Gloria said.

"I don't, either," I said.

That evening, The Gawgon was waiting in my room.

"So, Boy, you seem to have made an interesting decision. You lied to that lovely girl about going to England. Were you telling the truth this time? Do you really want to be an artist?"

I said I believed I did, and asked if she thought that was what I should be.

"My opinion is beside the point," said The Gawgon. "Don't

do something just because somebody else thinks it's a good idea."

I remarked that my father hoped I might work for the Pennsylvania Railroad.

"It's up to you," answered The Gawgon. "If you don't want to, then don't. That's what you told Gloria, isn't it?"

"Yes," I said, "I guess it was."

My father came up with yet another scheme to make our fortune: deodorizing public lavatories in office buildings, restaurants, gas stations, and department stores.

He designed a hollow cone that could be attached to the wall, and found someone to make plaster-of-paris castings of it. He bought a jug of concentrated perfume and, with a turkey baster, dripped a little into the cone. The perfume would seep out of the plaster and spread its aroma throughout the lavatory. He proposed selling the fixtures and charging for the service of going back and refilling them.

Each morning, he packed plaster cones, the jug of scent, and the turkey baster into a satchel and went into town hunting customers. Amazingly, he found some, and for a time, did make a little money. But he came home reeking of gardenias and had to change his clothes. Even then, the odor hung around the house.

"Phew! It smells like a New Orleans bardello," Aunt Rosie said, next time she visited.

"How would you know that?" my father said. When

she turned her back, he goosed her. Aunt Rosie gave a whoop.

"Oh, Alan," my mother said.

While my father grew heroically optimistic, I grew more agonized. Gloria's portrait was coming along well; coming along, that is, very slowly, so that we saw each other almost every day. Fourth of July passed without much celebration. Summer's lease was getting shorter, my vile secret would soon be revealed and nothing I could do about it. What I did, in fact, was: nothing. I did not breathe a word of going to England, what school, in what grade. Still, my preposterous lie gnawed at me; the calendar made my fate inescapable.

Worse, my mother had been talking with Mrs. Woods, the principal of Rosetree Elementary. I knew nothing of it until she sat me down at the dining-room table.

She began by telling me not to be upset, a good clue I was going to be extremely upset. There was, she said, some question about my grade when school started. My marks at Rittenhouse Academy were—she did not use the word "appalling," but it hovered around the edges. I had been out of school for such a long time, followed no approved studies, and as far as the official world reckoned it, I was deeply uneducated. A "savitch," as Aunt Rosie said.

"Mrs. Woods is a lovely person," my mother went on. "Very kind and sympathetic. But—and she was frank—she doubts that you'll qualify for sixth grade."

My mother gently exploded another bombshell:

"It's likely you'll have to repeat fifth grade. Possibly"—she hesitated, seeing my expression—"possibly you may go back to fourth. Mrs. Woods wants you to take a special test and she'll see."

I was, blessedly, too numb to remember much of what happened after that. My mother did take me to Rosetree Elementary. Mrs. Woods, as my mother said, was kindly and considerate, a smiling executioner. I sat at a desk along with some other victims. A couple of them were big, hulking boys who looked as if they had grown to manhood in fourth grade. We all had the hangdog air of educational felons.

Mrs. Woods passed out booklets and pencils and personally supervised the torture. It took a long time, though I marked down my answers as quickly as I could. At home again, I slunk to my garret. I wanted to see The Gawgon. She was not there.

I could only try to put the whole sorry affair out of my mind and fill my remaining days full of Gloria. I kept working on her portrait, which would never be finished. We rode our bicycles, we walked through the woods, we laughed, it was all wonderful and doomed.

For a time, I was able to forget what lay in store, but the closer we came to Labor Day, the heavier my secret weighed. I knew I would soon be forced to decide: wait like a coward until she found out, or bravely tell her myself. I preferred cowardly; for, if I said nothing, I could still hope to be run over by a truck.

That afternoon, Gloria and I were sitting on the Ormonds' lawn swing. It was warm yet. The Ormonds' big trees hadn't started changing.

I tried working on her portrait but erased what I had done. I had brought my story about the Aldinis and Ormondis. "For you to keep," I said. "You can read it when I'm not here." Then I said:

"I'm not going to England."

I did not confess out of heroic nobility. I couldn't carry the lie around with me anymore. I knew I would not be saved by a careening truck.

Gloria said she was glad I didn't have to go away.

Quickly, before I could change my mind, I said I was never going to England in the first place, not to Rugby or anywhere else. I wasn't even going to junior high. I'd be in elementary school and lucky if they put me in sixth grade instead of fourth or fifth.

Gloria stared at me. "You made it all up?"

I looked away and nodded. I did not try to explain. I had no idea how or what to explain.

Gloria got out of the swing and ran into the house. Mrs. Ormond was looking at me from the kitchen window. I got on the bicycle and went home.

I hardly slept that night. I had one more thing to do. In the morning, I rode back to her house. I had forgotten they would be getting ready for a weekend at the seashore. They were all in the driveway. Nick and Mr. Ormond packed things in the car. Gloria had just come out of the house. I wheeled the bicycle up to her.

"I'll put this in the garage," I said. "You'll want it back now."

"You don't have to do that," Gloria said. "I was mad, at first, because you lied to me. It doesn't matter. You were just being silly. The story was silly, too." Then she grinned. "I loved it."

She went on to tell me she didn't care what grade I'd be in. If we were in different schools, we could still see each other afternoons and weekends.

Mr. Ormond was calling for her to get moving.

"It won't make any difference," Gloria said.

I knew it would.

On Friday, my mother sat me down again at the dining-room table. She had a call from Mrs. Woods about the test. Mrs. Woods was troubled.

I said I guessed I had flunked. It did not surprise me.

My mother shook her head. "You got a good score. Better than good." That, my mother said, was what troubled Mrs. Woods. According to the test, I belonged in junior high. She didn't want to hold me back, but it was a big jump and Mrs. Woods worried I might not be ready for it. She thought it would be easier on me if I spent the year in sixth grade.

"She did say," my mother added, "whoever taught you must have been remarkable. That would have pleased Annie."

But, my mother added, I was the one to decide what I wanted to do.

For the sake of appearances, I thought it over for about three seconds. Seventh grade, I said, was fine with me.

Gloria would be glad to know. I would tell her as soon as she was home.

I went to the attic later. The Gawgon was sitting in her rocking chair.

"I'm glad you confessed to that ridiculous whopper," she said. "You at least cleared your conscience. Now there's room for the next foolish thing you do. And, I gather, you're moving up in the world."

I told The Gawgon I didn't care what grade I was in as long as Gloria and I could be together, sweethearts forever.

The Gawgon smiled. "Nothing is forever. But some things do last longer than others."

We sat quietly for some time. The Gawgon stood up.

"I'll go now," she said.

I asked when I would see her again, and hoped it would be soon.

"No, not soon," The Gawgon said fondly. "I did what I could for you. From now on, it's up to you. You have your own life to live. And I?" She laughed. "I'm dead, after all."

"Yes," I said. "I know that."

"Good." The Gawgon's face lightened. She had her same bright look of a girl.

Before she was gone, she turned and said:

"I'll not be back. Don't forget me."

"I won't," I said.

The Gawgon kept her word. She never came back. I kept mine. I never forgot.